boy shopping

boy shopping

NIA STEPHENS

Dafina Books for Young Readers
A Parachute Press Book
KENSINGTON PUBLISHING CORP.
http://www.kensingtonbooks.com

DAFINA BOOKS are published by

Kensington Publishing Corp.
850 Third Avenue
New York, NY 10022

ISBN-13: 978-0-7582-1929-9
ISBN-10: 0-7582-1929-6

First Kensington Trade Paperback Printing: April 2007
10 9 8 7 6 5 4 3 2

Printed in the United States of America

Acknowledgments

The author would like to thank Dr. Harvard Stephens and Dr. Barbara Nabrit-Stephens for their support (financial and otherwise); Larry David Woods and Cynthia Matthews; Paula Penn-Nabrit and family; Sharon Williams and the Paramore family; the Debater Grrl Kollektiv, especially Jacqueline Kirby and Mira De; the Codex Writers' Group, especially Judson Roberts; the Secret Writer's Club of Nashville; Juanita and Madeline of Dulce Desserts; and Laura Rennert.

Very special thanks are due to the friends who supplied cupcakes, coffee, pleasant distraction and general encouragement when I needed it: Tua Chaudhuri, Sarah Ribeiro, Beth Gilmore, Patrick Slusher, John A. B. Burton, Greg Harris, and George Metcalfe. And special thanks to Sara Lurie.

Chapter 1

Right Here, Right Now

Derrick the stage manager had cranked the footlights so high that everything beyond Kiki Kelvin's crash cymbal was a blur of blue and red lights. Every fourth beat during "Satisfy Me?" she slammed the crash, a sound loud enough to shake the old cinder-block walls that had absorbed the music of Nirvana, REM, and Garbage before Kiki and her friends treated them to the sounds of Temporary Insanity. She could feel the beat traveling up through the floorboards and into her bones, even into the long, shiny dreads whipping around her head. She was the beat, her heart slamming in time with her drums.

Kiki didn't have to see him to know that the lead singer, Franklin Pierce, was writhing center-stage, making the girls in the audience scream the chorus along with him. Mark Slaughter was a slim shadow somewhere to her left, leaning into his bass—the way she lunged into the drum kit, sitting a little closer than most drummers would. Of course, most drummers were guys. But that had never bothered Kiki, the other members of

Temporary Insanity, or the crowd rocking the Exit/In's foundations.

They always ended the set with "Satisfy Me?," Franklin growling out the lyrics as if he had written them. Franklin had no problem satisfying himself—with their groupies. Kiki was the one who "Just couldn't see/Which one of you is gonna satisfy me."

The girls in the audience thought the song was an invitation. Really, Kiki had written it as a joke about the skinny, pale, dopey-eyed boys who burned CDs for her, with titles like *Songs of Faith and Devotion*—like she didn't know that was a Depeche Mode album. Kiki needed a boyfriend who got the music but also knew she wasn't just a girl drummer in a rock band, someone who saw more than a heart-shaped face under gleaming dreads, and a lot more than the back of her vintage flares.

Someone like Mark, who was there at Café Momus the night she scribbled the lyrics for "Satisfy Me?" on a napkin and had helped her with the melody line. Mark, who drove her home after band practice in his Karmann Ghia, a funky old car that his dad bought when he was dating Mark's mom. Mark, who held out his hand so that Kiki could feel how tough his calluses had become from hours of practicing on his bass, leathery patches at the tips of long, thin fingers. Mark, who had the bluest eyes Kiki had ever seen, though his hair was even darker than hers, while his skin was the blue-white of skim milk and Kiki's was more like rich hot chocolate.

Kiki and Mark had been friends forever, long before Franklin transferred to the Wentworth Preparatory Academy, Nashville's most elite private school, and convinced them to form a band, back when her teachers still called her Katrina and her mom French-braided her hair every morning. Mark was her best friend, and he acted like nothing had ever changed between them, like she was still the little girl with braids and braces and he still had skinned knees and at least one black eye, and nobody else wanted to play with them because Kiki was black and Mark was a scholarship kid.

"Satisfy Me?" ended on a drum solo, and Kiki laid into the drums as if they had done her wrong, slamming them so hard her wrists would hurt the next morning. The whole audience clapped in tempo, and when she banged out the final beat, the crowd screamed with one voice for an encore before they had a chance to bow.

The three of them waved and dashed into the wings. Franklin's number-one groupie, Lizzie, handed each of them a bottle of water. It had taken them three months to teach Lizzie that even though Kiki was not technically a guy, she was still a part of the band. For some reason, Lizzie was the only one who seemed to notice that Kiki was a girl. Mark and Franklin were always surprised when Lizzie didn't offer Kiki a back rub or a cigarette like she did them, even though Mark didn't smoke. Neither did Kiki, who was just as glad that Lizzie had never offered her a massage, and would be even happier if Lizzie kept her hands off Mark, too.

"Feel up to one more?" Franklin asked them, lighting up. His eyes were the same pale gray as the smoke. With those eyes, platinum blond hair, and skin so clear most girls would kill for it, Kiki could understand why he had his own fan club on MySpace, even though she wouldn't go out with Franklin for anything. He was cute and he was fun, but he knew it all too well. And he thought he was too much fun for any one girl to keep all to herself.

"Sure," Mark said, glancing at Kiki for confirmation. They'd been friends so long they were practically psychic. Sometimes all they had to do was see one another across the hall to burst out laughing.

"My throat's kind of raw," Franklin admitted, taking another drag off his cigarette. "You want to do the new one?"

Mark had his head thrown back, gulping water, so Kiki said, "Let's do it."

As soon as Franklin was able to pry Lizzie's hands from his shoulders they went back on stage. The crowd, which had been stomping out the "We Will Rock You" beat, screamed and cheered as Franklin and Mark switched instruments and Kiki picked up her drumsticks.

"This is a new one for us," Mark purred into the microphone. It always weirded Kiki out, hearing the same voice she heard on the telephone every night amplified to one hundred decibels. "We were saving it for you."

It was an old song, actually, the last track on Depeche Mode's *Violator* album: "Blue Dress." Pretty and sad, Mark's gentle tenor caressed the lyrics. The one time Franklin sang it in practice, his bass rumble made the request to put on a beloved blue dress sound like an order.

As she tapped out the rhythm, Kiki wondered if she had some dress Mark preferred, something that someday he would beg her to wear. It seemed like everyone else had a favorite Kiki outfit—Derrick, the Exit/In's stage manager, liked the one she had on now: pin-striped short-shorts with pink suspenders, black velvet combat boots, fishnet stockings, and a

pink-and-black necktie. But Mark never seemed to notice anything she wore.

Derrick had turned the footlights low and bathed Mark in a
spotlight. Now Kiki could see the curve of his shoulders as he
cradled the Stratocaster, the blue highlights in his dark hair, and
when he glanced over his shoulder at Kiki she saw the shadows
under his blazing blue eyes, shadows he got from staying up all
night to finish his homework after band practice, or after shows.
She smiled, nodded, and kept the beat. So did the audience,
clapping in time. Lost in the groove, Kiki wanted the song to
go on and on forever. But she stopped on cue, blew kisses to
the audience, and made her way to her dressing room, ignoring Lizzie's offer of a towel. Drumming was sweaty work even
without stage lighting, but Kiki liked to pretend that Lizzie
didn't exist.

Kiki's friend Jasmine Ash was waiting for her backstage,
wearing an outfit that could have come from Kiki's closet, and
maybe had. She and Jasmine were tight, even though their per-
sonalities could not be more different. Kiki took everything
seriously: her music, her friendships, her rare moments of free
time. Jasmine couldn't be serious about anything for more than
five minutes. She would flirt for half an hour with a guy at a
club, make him think she was ready to jump in bed with him,
then for the next month she'd give out his phone number to
every guy who asked for her number. And unlike Kiki, who was
careful to watch her words in case there was a journalist around
somewhere, Jasmine always said exactly what she thought—
and Jasmine had a very dirty mind.

"So," Kiki asked, herding Jasmine into her tiny dressing
room. Green Room B was usually a storage area for spare equip-

ment, with just one swinging light bulb and a cracked mirror hanging over a dusty sink. Green Room A was a lot nicer, but that's where Mark and Franklin were changing. "Where's the party?"

"Sasha's."

"Oh, right!" Kiki exclaimed, unzipping the backpack she had crammed with post-show clothes. "Tonight's when we finally get to see Thomas."

"Five bucks says he's a troll."

"No deal." Not that Kiki really thought that Sasha would go out with someone completely hideous, but there had to be something wrong with Thomas. Sasha had been strangely secretive about him for weeks. They'd only found out Mystery Boy's name by snagging Sasha's cell phone one night after she fell asleep. They didn't even know how Sasha had met Thomas— he didn't go to Wentworth, and Sasha never went anywhere without Jasmine or Camille. She couldn't; she didn't know how to drive. Neither did Kiki. Wentworth didn't offer driver's ed, so they had to enroll in summer school to take it, but Sasha and Kiki had both been gone the entire summer. Sasha had gone on a tour of Europe with her grandmother, which was a lot less fun than she thought it would be, and Kiki was stuck on the tour bus with Mark, Franklin, their tour manager, Judy, and the bus driver, Bill—who hated musicians in general and teenage musicians in particular. Most of the time Franklin's mother had been around too, and between her yelling at Judy, Judy yelling at Bill, and Mark and Franklin yelling at each other, Kiki spent most of the summer wishing she were standing in line at European museums with Sasha's grandmother. And that was before the bus's toilet broke.

"Sure you don't want to ride with Mark?"

Kiki's fingers froze in the middle of lacing up the front of her lacy black bustier. "Are you joking?"

"But he's your *best friend*." There was a little edge to Jasmine's voice that told Kiki what this was really about. Whenever Kiki wasn't busy with the band, she and Jasmine shopped together, partied together, and even sometimes did their homework together—but Kiki always called Mark her best friend.

The truth was that Kiki was almost always busy with the band—and Mark was a huge part of that. Ever since they signed with RGB Records, the hipster division of one of the Big Three major labels, Kiki's life had become an endless series of recording sessions, photo shoots, gigs in the city during the school year, and touring all summer. The label had wanted all three band members to drop out of Wentworth and finish high school online so they could tour year-round, but Kiki's and Mark's parents had refused.

At the time, Kiki was ready to kill her parents—Nashville is full of people desperate for a contract, people who would literally do anything to get one. Franklin's parents were convinced that RGB would drop them and find some other teenage band to promote if the other parents kept making difficulties. In the end, though, Kiki was glad her parents had held out. It was Judy's job to keep all three members of Temporary Insanity from having anything like a social life when they were on tour, at least until each of them turned eighteen—Kiki wasn't even allowed to sit on the boys' beds, and vice versa. So her so-called life at Wentworth was all the social life she had.

"Things with Mark and me are a little complicated," Kiki admitted. "When we're together, I'm always wondering what he's really thinking. Does he know how I feel about him? Does he care? Is it even possible that he just doesn't know?" She gave her lacings a yank and tied them in a double knot. Her bustier was the real thing, vintage, all black velvet and white lace. It went with dark jeans and kitten heels perfectly.

Kiki had never understood why some people did all their shopping at the mall, where there were racks and racks full of clothes that looked exactly alike. The real thrill was vintage shopping, where every item was unique, with its own strange history. Kiki loved to prowl through vintage shops when she had a few hours off in a new city, in search of the one random item that felt like it had been made just for her, whether fifteen or fifty years before.

"Things between you and Mark aren't complicated enough," Jasmine countered. "Whatever you might hope is going to happen, and maybe it *is* going to happen someday, when pink ponies come flying out of my ass, at the moment you two are just friends."

"You've got a point." Kiki peered into the cracked mirror at the back of Green Room B. When she was onstage, she couldn't think of anything better than rocking out every night for years to come. But between shows, when she was dressing for a party where all the boys would be spooked by the fact that she had a half-million-dollar recording contract—except for Franklin and Mark, who considered her off-limits anyway—Kiki sometimes wondered if it was worth it.

"You look fantastic," Jasmine said, smiling over Kiki's shoulder. With her tiny, sharp face surrounded by wild red hair, Jasmine looked almost demonic. There were rumors going around Wentworth that Jasmine was a witch, based mostly on her devilish hair color and her tendency to lob insults that burned like battery acid. Kiki knew that Jasmine was no witch, but her smile was positively wicked. "Let's party."

Sasha Silverman's house was the best kind for parties, at least when the weather was warm: south of the city proper, surrounded by woods. Her parents had gone to New York for the Bennie awards—the Oscars for country music—like half the Wentworth parents, so there would be parties every night for the next few days. Not that Kiki would be able to go to most of them; part of her agreement with her parents for sign-ing the deal was that she would never go out on school nights past 10:30 unless she had a gig, and she was only allowed one weeknight gig a month. Her weekend curfew was 2:00 sharp unless she was spending the night at a friend's house. If she weren't in a band, she'd have a lot more freedom.

"Maybe Thomas is in the mob or something," Jasmine guessed as she pulled up behind Mark's Kharmann Ghia. As usual, the guys had finished loading out the instruments and left the club long before Kiki had finished getting dressed. They were at the end of a long line of cars. Kiki recognized most of them from the Wentworth parking lot.

Sasha's house, set almost half a mile from the road, looked like an alien starship that crashed into a Tennessee meadow, all weirdly curved bits of silver metal and windows in sur-prising places. Like a lot of music industry types, the Silver-mans were originally from LA, and they didn't want anyone to forget it.

"The closest thing we've got to the mob in Nashville is the MuzikMafia, and I don't think Sasha would sleep with anyone

9

who wore a cowboy hat," Kiki said, kicking off her heels, preparing for the long hike across the lawn.

"What about you? Cowboy Troy is pretty hot."

Kiki almost threw a shoe at her. "I don't date anybody who sings country music, black or not."

"He doesn't sing, he raps country," Jasmine explained as they got out of the car. "They call it hick-hop."

"Are you kidding? No, don't answer that." They set out, watching their steps carefully by moonlight. The Silvermans didn't keep horses, but they did have dogs. Big dogs. Despite the danger of stepping in something gross, it was a perfect night for a long walk, barefoot in wet grass. October is still warm in Nashville most years, and this was no exception. Kiki was daydreaming about her Halloween costume while Jasmine went on and on about the night she and Camille met Cowboy Troy at a party Laura Keller's parents threw.

"You could do a lot worse than him," Jasmine decided. "And it's not like you're otherwise involved."

"I'm always 'otherwise involved,'" Kiki pointed out, plucking a late-season daisy to wear over her ear. "Where do you think I was when you were partying with Cowboy Troy?"

"You were working!"

"Playing a show isn't really work." The photo shoots, interviews, rehearsals, meeting with reps, lawyers, and managers—that was work. But actually being onstage making music was different for Kiki. Playing music really was play.

Jasmine rolled her eyes. Her parents were entertainment lawyers, and she shared their belief that music was just something to buy and sell, like soap or legal services. They might like being lawyers, but they wouldn't do it for free. The fact that

Kiki would play music for free—would, in fact, pay for the right to play—just seemed crazy to Jasmine's whole family.

"That wasn't my point anyway," Jasmine said.

"You had a point?"

Jasmine snapped the bloom off another daisy and threw it at Kiki. "My point is, when was the last time you went out on a date?"

"Mark and I rented a movie to watch while we did a physics problem set Thursday night."

"If you think that's a date, then it's been too long."

"It felt like a date. Sort of. I mean, we were in his bed." Sprawling across Mark's battered old quilt, so faded it was almost white, doodling on his ankle with a Sharpie while he figured out when two trains, hurtling at each other along the same track, would crash—it felt so *right*. Just thinking about it made Kiki's chest hurt. How could he not feel it?

"*On* his bed. With physics books and graphing calculators. Come on, Kiki—when was the last time a guy took you to dinner, then to a party?"

"Last Saturday."

Jasmine groaned dramatically, like a sick cow. Still, Kiki could barely hear her over the pounding bass of "Gold Digger" thudding from Sasha's house. They were close enough now to see dancing shadows inside one of the second-floor rooms.

"Kiki, when your managers take you to dinner to go over contracts, then drag you to a label meet-and-greet, that is not a date! When was the last time a guy—not a manager, not a reporter, not Mark or Franklin—a *real* guy asked you out?"

"Guys ask me out every day." Usually the same guys, every day. The ones who had Temporary Insanity bumper stickers all over their lockers, even though Wentworth fined $100 per sticker at the end of the year because it was so hard to remove them.

"I said real guys! Stupid loser stalker types who are just into you because of the band don't count!"

"This conversation is over," Kiki said, stepping from the wild lawn to the concrete porch.

"Kiki, you need to get over it. Mark isn't the only guy in the world, and if he doesn't want you like you want him, then—"

"Hey!" Sasha yelled, kicking open the front door. She had a bottle of Southern Comfort in her left hand and an antique telescope in her right. Her tiny dress was made of black patent leather and her toenails were painted to match, which made her skin look even paler than it was. But her cheeks were flushed from dancing and dimpled by her huge smile.

"You've got great timing," Kiki said, giving her a hug.

As always, Sasha's violet curls smelled like Christmas, a mixture of clove cigarettes and vanilla shampoo. Sasha was the sweetest person Kiki knew, much nicer than Kiki was herself, and gorgeous, too—she was the only goth Kiki had ever met who didn't need makeup to create flawless skin and blood-red lips. But Sasha had as much trouble with Wentworth boys as Kiki did, and for the same reason: they found her intimidating.

Boys saw the black clothes, angel face, and purple hair and assumed that Sasha Silverman was wild and dangerous. They all seemed to think that Sasha would only date equally dark, poetic boys in long black trench coats, though Sasha would have been happy to date any of the geeky, quiet boys who were too afraid to talk to her. Instead, her freshman year she went out with a junior named Jake, who was too dumb to be intimidated by her, and a senior named Ben the next, who wasn't stupid, but wasn't half as smart as he thought he was. Sasha had put up with each of them for six months, then dumped them when she decided it was better to be single and lonely than lonely in a relationship.

"Darling, I've got great *everything*," she said in her mother's fake old-Hollywood accent, then she cracked up. Her giggles rose above the thudding bass coming from—well, Kiki wasn't sure where it was coming from. Every room was wired for sound, but she guessed that most people were dancing in the living room, off to the left. Her guess was confirmed when a tall, thin stranger came staggering from that direction with a recycling bin full of empty bottles.

"Thomas, you don't have to do that!" Sasha said, whirling around. Jasmine's jaw dropped, but Kiki had to laugh, and kick herself for not taking Jasmine's bet. Thomas was gorgeous— gorgeous!—but not at all what Kiki expected. He was black, for one thing, with skin the color of wildflower honey, and dark gold eyes like the harvest moon. And instead of gothic black, he was wearing a rose-red shirt and dark jeans, an outfit that Kiki knew hadn't come from any mall in Nashville.

"I don't mind at all. But where shall I empty it?" This time, Kiki's mouth fell open. Thomas's low, velvety voice, which could put Franklin's to shame, was made even more irresistible by a crisp British accent.

"I'll take it," Sasha said, trying to pull the heavy bin from his grasp without setting down her drink or her telescope. "You're not supposed to lift a finger. You're my guest. I order you to go have fun!"

"The kitchen's that way," Kiki told Thomas, waving him toward the back of the house. She and Jasmine each grabbed one of Sasha's elbows and dragged her to the nearest bathroom for interrogation.

"So what do you think?" Sasha asked, perched on the sink. She was giggling because she knew exactly what Kiki and Jasmine thought.

"I think he has a twin brother," Jasmine said as she checked to make sure the door was locked. "At least, he'd better."

"Set of triplets?" Kiki asked hopefully.

"'Fraid not. One and only. Rarer than a black rose is beauty such as his. A blossom among the thorns—" She suddenly hiccupped, which was a good thing, because Kiki could see that Sasha could probably spout gothic love poetry all night about Thomas.

"Did you meet him during the summer?" Jasmine's voice had gone squeaky with amazement.

"I *wish*. Touring churches with Grandma would have been a lot more fun if I had known he was waiting for me back at the hotel."

"So where did he come from?"

"London."

"You know that's not what I mean!"

"Oh, right. He's an exchange student, over at Carroll Academy."

"What were you doing at Carroll?" It was an all-boys prep school that beat Wentworth year after year in football. That annual game was the only time Wentworth students saw the Carroll boys. Carroll had a sister school, called Quincy Hall, that shared Carroll's dances and drama department.

"I didn't meet him at Carroll. What difference does it make how we met?" Sasha was blushing again, and not from happiness. Kiki wondered what the big secret could possibly be, since Thomas was not a member of the mafia or the Muzik-Mafia, and definitely was not a troll.

"Um, hello—who is single here? Is it everyone? We need information!" Jasmine pointed out.

"Oh, I don't think you'd really be interested in how I met Thomas."

"Are you kidding?" Jasmine squealed. "Sasha—"

All three of their cell phones suddenly beeped.

"Camille," they all said, before they even checked to see the text message. Of course it was Camille, asking them, *Where y'at?*

While Jasmine tried to explain which of Sasha's seven bathrooms they were in (in fewer than one hundred and twenty-five letters), Kiki watched Sasha stare at the door. She had never seen Sasha so happy about a guy. Yes, she was drunk, but Kiki had seen Sasha drunk around Jake and Ben, the two guys she had gone out with before, and it wasn't the same. Sasha was always slightly different around Ben and Jake, a little too quiet, not as giggly, not as confident. Sasha would never have ordered them to go have fun, even in jest.

"So what's up with you and Thomas?" Kiki finally asked.

Sasha gazed down at her, with nothing but happiness in her gray eyes.

"I am in love. At long last. Sasha, Queen of Loneliness, has found the one."

"How do you know he's the one?" asked Jasmine.

A loud banging on the door kept Sasha from answering. Jasmine unlocked the door and let in Camille.

"Thought you could use these," Camille said, handing around icy cans of Diet Coke. They each poured an inch or two into the sink, then made up the difference with Southern Comfort.

Anyone at Wentworth would say that Kiki, Jasmine, Sasha, and Camille were the hottest girls in the junior class. People called them the Pussycat Posse, even though that annoyed all four of them, especially Kiki—she'd rather be compared to a band with some musical talent than to the Pussycat Dolls. Still, whether they liked it or not, the name stuck and the girls managed to make it their own. Sometimes, though, Kiki was curious how Camille got lumped in with them. She was the only one who was pretty in an ordinary, everyday sort of way, so she was the only one the boys felt comfortable with. They might want to sleep with all four of them, but they only wanted to date Camille.

"So . . . how do you know he's the one?" Jasmine repeated after taking a swig of her drink.

"You know the perfect fit when you feel it," Camille answered for Sasha. "Same with jeans as it is with boys."

"*You* know how they got together," Jasmine said accusingly.

Kiki knew Jasmine was right: Sasha must have told Camille the truth about Thomas. Camille was more likely to compare boys to video games (fun when they're new, uninteresting once you win them) or cake (tasty, but bad for you) than to clothes. Kiki, Jasmine, and Sasha would use the clothes comparison, but not Camille. That *had* to be a comparison Camille picked up from Sasha.

Sasha gave Camille a piercing glare.

"I didn't say anything!" Camille squealed in self-defense.

"You know you're going to tell us sooner or later, so spill it," Jasmine said.

Sasha pursed her lips, but Jasmine's icy glare finally got to her.

She threw her head back, took a sip from her spiked soda, then exploded. "All right! I met him online!" She finished off her drink, then glared at Kiki and Jasmine. "Go ahead! Laugh!"

Kiki met Jasmine's eyes in the mirror and raised her eyebrows. Jasmine's jaw had dropped. Kiki knew just how she felt. She had always thought that online dating was for old maids desperately searching for someone to marry, not gorgeous teenagers like Sasha and Thomas.

"We're not laughing, Sash," Kiki said thoughtfully. "I mean, yeah, we wouldn't want you going out with some old perv you met on MySpace, but Thomas . . . Thomas . . ."

"Thomas is hotter than a biscuit! You met him online?" Jasmine squealed in amazement. "Where?"

"There's this site, called HelloHello. These girls I know from the gym told me about it. It's not like MySpace. You have to be invited to get on by two people who're already members . . . that keeps the pervs off. Most people on the Nashville site are in private schools, which makes sense—most of us have been going to school with the same seventy-five people since kindergarten, and it's hard to meet people outside of school. But it's not just a dating site. You can post what you want—pictures, profile, whether you're just there to connect with people in your area, or if you're looking for love or whatever. And you just shop, sort of, for what you're looking for. It's fun."

"I think it's awesome," Camille said, sliding her arm around Sasha's waist. "Can you and Thomas invite me?"

"Of course!" Sasha said.

Jasmine gaped at Camille. "Why would you need to look online for a guy? Everybody wants to go out with you!"

Camille shrugged. "I've already gone out with everyone datable at Wentworth."

They all laughed, though it wasn't strictly true.

"What about Franklin?" Kiki asked. "He's hot." Kiki knew that Franklin would go out with Camille in a heartbeat.

Camille's nose wrinkled. "Franklin is probably crawling with disease. Definitely not Franklin."

"You haven't gone out with Mark," Jasmine pointed out, grinning evilly at Kiki in the mirror.

"Kiki's Mark? Are you kidding?"

"Yes, she's kidding." Kiki punched Jasmine in the shoulder. She screeched as if Kiki had stabbed her.

"What's the holdup with Mark now?" Camille asked. That was a sign of how drunk she was—they had had a million conversations about Mark's inability to see Kiki as anything other than a bandmate and a friend.

Kiki, Jasmine, and Sasha all sighed.

"No, I know all about Judy the tour-bitch and how you can't get together on tour, and how he somehow failed to notice that you've turned into a total hottie over the years." Camille rolled her eyes. "But what's stopping you from marching into the game room right now, dragging him away from the pool table, and telling him what he's missing? Why don't you just ask him out?"

"What do you mean?" Kiki said. "I ask him out all the time!"

"Not out for coffee at that greasy, all-night place you like,"

Camille said. "*Out* out. Ask him to a show, no Franklin, no groupies, no us—ask him to take you to the movies! Anything! Just make sure he knows it'll be a date."

"But then he'll say no."

"No, he won't. He'll kick himself for being so stupid for the last three years."

Kiki shook her head. "No way. I know him a lot better than you do. He has to feel like everything is his idea. It'll weird him out completely if I make the first move." It was one of the very few things that annoyed her about Mark, along with his unwillingness to notice her as anything other than a best friend.

"Then you can go out with Cowboy Troy," Jasmine pointed out.

"Huh?" Sasha asked.

Camille waved her soda can at Jasmine. "Jazz, *you* need to call Cowboy Troy. You've been talking about him for months. And Kiki, you need to either ask Mark out or get over it. He's getting in your way."

"He's not stopping me from going out with other people. I went out with Jason Wrightman for most of last year."

"You know you never really gave him a chance."

Kiki couldn't argue with that. The lead singer of Beautiful Youth was cute, smart, and hilarious, and he understood the demands of a musician's schedule perfectly. But between his gigs and Kiki's, they barely managed to see each other, and when they did Kiki always wished that Mark liked her half as much as Jason did. Kiki even slept with Jason a few times, mostly because she hoped making love would make her fall in love, but it never happened. They never even broke up, not really—they just drifted apart, Kiki with the Wasted tour, and Jason heading to the European festival circuit. She missed talking to him on the phone, but that was all she missed.

"You can do it," Jasmine told Kiki firmly. "You can ask Mark out. And if he says no, forget him. The Internet is full of Thomases."

"There's only one Thomas," Sasha corrected her. "But the Internet *is* full of boys. We'll find the right one for you."

"But I don't want some random boy!" Kiki wailed. "I want Mark!"

"Then go and get him."

Jasmine took the drink from Kiki's hand and replaced it with lipstick: Hearts Afire, Kiki's signature red. Jasmine always kept a tube in her purse for Kiki, since Kiki could never remember to bring a purse of her own. Kiki applied it carefully, fluffed her dreads, and took a deep breath.

"Okay, that's it. I'm going to find Mark, and when I do, I'm going to ask him out for real."

"Go, Kiki, go!" her friends chanted.

Kiki set off down the hall, which seemed to be heading downhill. That was weird, because it was pretty level on the way to the bathroom. Drinking on an empty stomach was bad enough, but after a show she was always a little dehydrated, which made any drink seem twice as strong.

"Dutch courage," she mumbled to herself, wondering what was with the Dutch. Dutch courage. Going Dutch. Double Dutch. What did it even mean? Mark's mom was Dutch. *She* liked Kiki—she gave her a pair of wooden shoes when she was eight. What was wrong with Mark?

Kiki careened into the game room. It was packed with people, mostly guys, and strangely quiet—a lot of Wentworth guys were serious about pool. Crowded as it was, Kiki knew immediately that Mark wasn't there. It was like a super power: Mark-sense. She would rather be able to fly.

"Seen Mark?" she asked Charles Anderson, who was standing closest to the door. When they were in the first grade, Charles had tried to cut off one of Kiki's pigtails. He told their teacher that he was trying to do her a favor—that maybe her hair would grow back "pretty." Straight was what he meant. But now he was as awed by Kiki as everyone else. He turned purple before he managed to stutter out the news that Mark had gone home right after Camille beat him at Seven Shot.

"Great," Kiki sighed, and turned back to the door.

"Do you need a ride somewhere?" piped a voice somewhere behind her.

"No thanks." Kiki headed for the first empty guest room she could find and crawled into bed. She would see Mark at noon the next day for a recording session. They were covering an old David Bowie song for a tribute album, but she couldn't ask him out in front of Franklin, Franklin's mother, their managers, the sound technicians, and everyone else at the studio. And that night, she would be locked in her bedroom, finishing a paper on *The Scarlet Letter*. She always saw Mark after homeroom, when she was headed to AP English and he was going to Calc.

"I'll talk to him on Monday," she promised herself before falling asleep.

✳ *Chapter 2* ✳
Temporary Insanity

Kiki dressed carefully on Monday morning. Wentworth didn't have uniforms, but it did have a dress code, and it banned almost all of her clothes. She chose skinny jeans long enough to hide her four-inch-high boot heels, and a black turtleneck made of a shiny, stretchy material that clung to her curves. There wasn't a bare inch of skin from neck to toe, once she added black lace gloves she had inherited from her grandmother, but it was a decidedly sexy outfit.

"You're pushing it, sweetheart," her mother said, dropping her off at school. "What's Dr. Eckhart going to say about that top?"

"Nothing. I've got the dress code memorized," Kiki promised.

"Have fun in court!"

Her mother made a face that kept Kiki giggling until she got to homeroom. Her mother had been a judge since Kiki was twelve, one of the first black women to win a seat on the bench in Nashville. Kiki always worried about someone she knew being arraigned in her mother's courtroom, but it had never happened. When you were in the music business it was nice to have a mother who knew contract law like some mothers knew brownie recipes.

"Talked to Mark—" Sasha began before Mr. Hooper shushed them. Kiki shook her head and started riffling through her bag for a pen. Passing notes with Sasha was her daily activity during morning announcements. But after the first bell, they didn't hear Dr. Eckhart say, "Good morning, Lions. This is Monday, October 12th, and these are your morning announcements" as they all expected. Instead, a very familiar drum solo tore out of the PA system at high volume, followed by Franklin's voice howling, "Monday morning's for the weak/Bankers, teachers, other freaks/I'm gonna sleep until Friday/ When the bad kids come out to play."

Kiki froze in shock as every face in the room turned to her. "Friday Night Special" was followed by screams from a crowd. That didn't surprise Kiki—they had just debuted "Friday Night Special" at the Exit/In that Saturday. When the recorded cheers died down, "Mr. Sprinkles" blared, then clips of "Glitterbug," "Sky High," and Temporary Insanity's version of the jazz standard "How High the Moon." Kiki sang Ella Fitzgerald's part on that one, with Franklin doing a very odd interpretation of Charlie Parker.

She expected "Demonique" to come up next—it came after "Sky High" on their newest set list—but instead there was silence. Before Sasha had time to ask Kiki what they were doing on the announcements, Dr. Eckhart was on the PA.

"Franklin Pierce, Mark Slaughter, and Katrina Kelvin, please come to the office immediately. Everyone else, please proceed to first period. Homeroom is dismissed."

* * *

"I suppose you have some sort of explanation," Dr. Eckhart said once Temporary Insanity had gathered in her office, lined up in three hard-backed, wooden chairs. Dr. Eckhart was one of the first women to graduate from Wentworth, and Kiki sometimes wondered if the woman's blood had turned Wentworth blue. She was a little too obsessed with school traditions and order and whether there were bumper stickers on the lockers, and her punishments were sometimes frighteningly creative. For her third dress code violation, Kiki had had to wear the Wentworth uniform from 1952 for a month—and Wentworth was not coed in 1952.

But Dr. Eckhart was also fair. She always gave you a chance to defend yourself before deciding on your punishment. Unfortunately, Kiki had no idea who had hijacked the PA system, and no idea how they had done it. And she was pretty sure that Mark and Franklin couldn't explain it either.

"You three are very quiet," Dr. Eckhart observed. "Usually I can't persuade you to close your mouths."

"Dr. Eckhart, it's not our fault," Mark blurted. "We had nothing to do with it." His knuckles had gone white, gripping the chair. Kiki wasn't surprised. He worked hard to keep his scholarship, and if he got kicked out during the fall of his junior year, especially over something as stupid as this prank, Kiki was afraid he might kill himself.

"I confess that I can't think of any reason why you might choose such a dubious method of self-promotion."

"Um, right," Franklin said, glancing at Kiki to make sure he had understood Dr. Eckhart. "I mean, we've got promoters and stuff. And everyone here has already heard us play."

Dr. Eckhart stared at each of them silently for almost a minute. Kiki wondered if she and the boys would be Dr. Eckhart's slaves before school every morning for the next month, or something even worse. Finally, the principal spoke.

"You're quite correct, Franklin. So what do you imagine was the offender's motivation?"

"What?"

Mark rolled his eyes, forcing Kiki to stifle a laugh. She was a little giddy with relief. "She wants to know who did it, Franklin."

"Oh! Just a groupie," Franklin said, tossing back his hair and sliding lower in his chair. "I've got to get those girls in line."

Dr. Eckhart raised a pair of brows so white they were almost invisible. "For every female student I've fined for Temporary Insanity bumper stickers, I have fined three of their male classmates. Kiki, do you have any idea which of your fans might have tampered with my public address system?"

"Not really." Kiki shrugged and tried to look unconcerned, but her mind was racing, trying to decide which of her fans might be responsible. She thought Dr. Eckhart was probably right: this didn't seem like fangirl behavior. Girls tried to get Franklin's attention by giving him kudos on MySpace and dancing next to the stage at shows. Kiki couldn't imagine one of them deciding to impress Franklin by hacking the PA system. She also had a hard time believing that any of them were smart enough to pull it off.

Mark interrupted her thoughts by saying, "Franklin's right. It's more likely to be a girl. Kiki doesn't really have her own fans. Our guy fans are fans of the band, not Kiki specifically."

"Excuse me?" Kiki said, not sounding half as mad as she felt. Or as hurt. "What would you know about that?"

"I talked to that PR guy, Mike, about fan demographics," Mark explained mildly, as if he hadn't just insulted her. "He says that fans never key in on drummers. The guys who listen to the White Stripes aren't listening because they like Meg. Think about it—no one's ever into the drummer."

Kiki stared at Mark, too stunned to say a word. That was what he really thought? No wonder he'd never asked her out.

"Maybe it's that Katie girl," Franklin said thoughtfully, working the fingers of his left hand as if he was doing chord progressions. He did that on the rare occasions when he tried to use his brain. "Katie Fulsome. She seems smart."

"You only think she's smart because she wears glasses," Mark pointed out. He leaned forward in his seat. "I have no idea who it could be," he told Dr. Eckhart.

"Then I suppose you should go to class," Dr. Eckhart said slowly. "However, if you should learn any facts related to this morning's incident, I would like to hear about it."

"Of course!" Kiki promised. Mark nodded and Franklin added, "Sure thing." Then they left the office as fast as they could without actually running.

"You don't think Katie's smart?" Franklin asked once they were in the hallway outside the office.

"No!" Kiki and Mark both growled.

"Her bra size changes at every single show!" Mark said. "What's your problem?" Franklin demanded.

"My problem is that one of your stupid fans got us in trouble with Dr. Eckhart. I need her to write recommendations," Mark said, biting off each of his words.

"Kiki, are you worried about recommendations too?" Franklin asked in a fake, sugary voice.

"Nope." Her father was chief of neurosurgery at Vanderbilt University, which meant she'd have a full ride there if she got in. And her parents' strict rule that getting more than one B in any six week period would mean having to quit the band, had kept her on the principal's honor list since freshman year. Getting into college was one thing she didn't have to worry about—balancing college with touring, however, was a whole other story. "That's not the problem."

"So what's your damage?" Franklin sneered. "Are you jealous?"

"Of your deranged fans?" Kiki retorted. "I don't think so! But I am amazed that you could be stupid enough to think that one of your little idiots did this!"

Franklin smirked, and did his patented hair toss again. "When was the last time some guy threw his boxers on stage for you?"

"Fanboys don't do that to get attention, dumb-ass! They send CDs to my parents' house and flowers and cow hearts on Valentine's Day! Did you hear the sound quality on that recording? That was serious equipment—professional grade. Any of your fans with that kind of money would spend it on hooker clothes, not micro-recorders!"

"Look who's talking!" Mark shouted before Franklin could think up an answer. "Maybe if you didn't dress like that, maybe you wouldn't have to worry about crazy stalkers!"

Kiki was so stunned she couldn't answer. She could barely breathe. Her clothes were definitely sexy, but compared to most girls in the industry, she looked like a nun. Mark's face was almost as red as Kiki's lipstick, and he was panting as if he had just run a mile, but he kept yelling anyway. "What do you mean, cow hearts on Valentine's Day? Who's sending you that crap?"

"What do you care?" she screamed back. "You think anyone who plays the drums is a loser!"

"Back into the office, please," a stern voice behind them ordered. Kiki shut her eyes for a moment. They should definitely have gotten farther away from Dr. Eckhart's office before they started lobbing insults.

They followed Dr. Eckhart meekly. Kiki couldn't stop trembling, even though Dr. Eckhart sat in complete silence for five full minutes, waiting for someone to say something.

Once again, it was Mark who broke the silence. "I'm sorry," he mumbled. "That was my fault."

"Indeed? I was sure I heard more than one voice shouting."

"I'm sorry, too," Kiki immediately echoed. And she was. She could not remember the last time she was so sorry.

Dr. Eckhart tapped her fingertips together lightly. "You know, I've said from the beginning that you were too young for the responsibilities a band entails. Your grades haven't fallen, so I haven't complained too much, but shouting matches in the middle of first period are difficult to condone."

"It's not really our fault," Franklin insisted. "It's all because of the announcement thing." He shrank a little into the chair, then asked, "Are you going to suspend us?"

"The zero-tolerance policy on fighting does not apply to verbal violence, so the answer is no. But I may have to speak to your parents tonight. You are far too old for this sort of nonsense."

Franklin perked up, but Kiki and Mark slumped in despair. They didn't have a lot of freedom, and they were both certain that a little more would soon be taken away. Their only hope was that something even worse would happen over the course of the day, distracting Dr. Eckhart before she began her daily round of phone calls.

"Go to class," Dr. Eckhart ordered, and they fled.

"Kiki—" Mark began as soon as they left the office.

"Don't talk to me," she said. She wouldn't even turn to face him as she fast-walked down the corridor. "I don't want to hear it."

"Okay," he said slowly. "But after school—"

"I'll get a ride with someone else," she snapped.

"Oh. Well—"

"Leave. Me. Alone." Each word was punctuated with the sharp click of high heels on tile.

When lunchtime rolled around, Sasha, Jasmine, and Camille were waiting for Kiki at her locker, concerned expressions on their faces. No one said a word as Kiki spun the combination on her lock.

"You heard?" Kiki asked, pulling a vintage Pink Floyd lunch box full of leftovers out of her locker.

"I think everyone heard," Jasmine said, patting Kiki awkwardly on her shoulder. Jasmine was never as comfortable trying to make someone feel good as she was making people feel bad. "So I guess you're not going to practice tonight, huh?"

Kiki didn't say anything, just felt her cheeks warm. She might not have screamed her last words to Mark, but she hadn't whispered them either. She had no doubt that the whole school knew about their fight by now.

"We're going to get our nails done after school," Sasha interjected, giving Jasmine a dark look. "Want to come with us?"

"Nope." Kiki fanned her fingers for the girls, displaying her super-short nails. They had to be, otherwise she broke them hefting her drum kit in and out of the van. Of course Sasha knew this—she'd only invited Kiki to be kind.

"I'll get a ride home with my dad." Kiki sighed, and Sasha took the hint to change the subject. Sasha told a long story about talking on the phone with her dad on Sunday morning, pretending everything was under control at the house, while scraping vomit off the kitchen floor with a bag of ice tied to her head all after Kiki had gone home. It was a funny story, but Kiki didn't feel like laughing.

What was Mark thinking? Did he really think that Kiki dressed like a slut? How *could* he, when he knew that she had gotten into a fight with the style consultant over her refusal to wear any skirt short enough to flash the audience, any top cut so low that she couldn't wear a bra, and anything that showed her navel? There was a fine line between sexy and slutty, but Kiki knew which side of the line she was on—didn't Mark?

And how did that make any sense, considering his other comment that nobody was interested in drummers? She'd heard drummer jokes since her very first show, usually some variation on, "What do you call someone who wants to hang out with musicians? A groupie? No, a drummer!" Was it that hard to believe that guys liked her, just because she didn't play an instrument with strings? Did he think that any guy who liked her was a crazy stalker? For the first time since they were five, Kiki had no idea what Mark was thinking.

* Chapter 3 *

Boy Shopping

"You don't look so good, baby girl," Kiki's dad said when he pulled up in front of Wentworth, staring at her over the top of his new black-rimmed bifocals. Kiki thought they made him look like Denzel Washington as Malcom X, which Dr. Kelvin considered one of the nicest compliments he had ever received.

"Thanks, Dad. How was work?"

"Fine. What's up with you? Aren't you supposed to be going to Franklin's for practice?"

"Practice was cancelled." Of course, she didn't know if Franklin and Mark felt up to playing music, but she was definitely not in the mood. If they didn't appreciate her, they could find a drum machine somewhere.

"Those boys getting on your nerves?"

Kiki raised an eyebrow. Rumors spread fast at a school as small as Wentworth, but she didn't think they could reach the neurosurgery department at Vanderbilt in less than a day.

He laughed. "Any girl who was stuck with my friends in

high school, morning, noon, and night, would have stabbed every one of us. Teenaged boys are just stupid. It's the hormones."

"Maybe you can do a study on that, proving that seventeen-year-old boys can't think at all."

"You can't practice neurosurgery on a subject that doesn't have a brain. There's nothing to dissect."

She had to laugh at that. "You know, I've been thinking about what you said before I went on tour last summer."

"That I would cut off Franklin's hands if he touched you?"

She snorted at that. "I told you then that that would never happen."

"That if I heard you smoked anything I'd lock you in the basement until your eighteenth birthday?"

"Not that either. You said that you would support me with the music thing as long as I wanted to do it. But if I ever wanted to quit, you'd support me in that, too."

He raised his eyebrows. "Your mother is the one who can help you get out of the contract."

"I know. But you won't freak out about me letting my label down after they've spent a fortune promoting us, throwing away an opportunity that a lot of people would kill to have?" That was what her managers told her every time she complained about anything. And despite the fact that her managers were white, barely thirty, and slightly crazy, both of them reminded her of her father. Part of that was the way they treated her: like their favorite person in the whole world, unless she did something that annoyed them. Then she had to listen to lecture after lecture until they settled down.

"If you ask me to, I'll burn your drum kit in the backyard. It would be nice to have you around during the summer."

Kiki's heart fluttered at the thought of her drums on fire, the glittery red paint on the sides bubbling and turning black. No. No matter what happened between her and Mark, she would never give up music.

"Thanks, Dad."

"No problem." He grinned, and couldn't help adding, "The day I complain because you won't be spending all your time with a couple of boys is the day I need my own brain examined."

Once they got home, Kiki's dad asked her if she wanted to go out for dinner, since her mother was stuck doing paperwork at the courthouse.

"I've got a lot of homework," she said, trudging up to her room. It was true—she always had a lot of homework—but she didn't feel like doing it. Instead she logged into the Internet to check her e-mail. She still talked to lots of people she had toured with over the summer—not all the time, since they all had strange schedules, but she tried to check in at least once a week.

After laughing at Annette's description of a terrifying dinner full of mysterious, slimy objects, hosted by her Japanese label's reps, and Colin's complaints about adjusting to real life after ten months on the road, Kiki felt a little better. Good enough that when Franklin's number appeared on her cell phone, she actually answered. He might be calling to apologize—about as likely as him bringing a girl flowers—but anything could happen.

"Did you forget about practice?" His usual bass rumble had gone high and whiny.

"Nope. I'm just not coming."

"You have to come. We have to arrange the rhythm section for 'Every Angel,' and we've got to finish 'Foxfire.'"

"I don't have to do anything, Franklin, and I'm not going to until you and Mark say you're sorry."

"Sorry? Sorry for what?"

"Sorry you're just that stupid, maybe?"

"Look, Kiki, just 'cause you've got PMS, or haven't gotten laid in the last year, doesn't mean—"

Kiki hung up before she started screaming at him so loud that it might kill her cell phone. Whenever she disagreed with him, no matter how wrong he was, he always said it was PMS, or she wasn't getting laid. You'd think even Franklin would figure out that no one had PMS for a month straight, but his math skills were even worse than hers. She ignored the call when he instantly rang her back, concentrating instead on the text message she was typing to Sasha, Camille, and Jasmine.

Thru w. Mark & Frnkln 4ever. What r u up 2?

Before she could hit "send," she heard the asthmatic chug of Mark's Karmann Ghia coming up the hill. She scanned her bedroom for something to throw—her windows had a clear view of the front walk. There were books, but her mother would kill her for throwing anything with words in it. She had a few million pairs of shoes, but if she missed they might get dirty, and she liked her shoes. Then there were instruments: bongo drums, spare snares, cymbals, and hi-hats, and a keyboard she was teaching herself to play. Any one of them would hurt like hell, tumbling down from two stories, but she would never mistreat an instrument like that. She decided to run downstairs and tell her father to say she wasn't home, but she wasn't fast enough—she glimpsed Mark passing the big picture window in the living room, and that meant that he saw her.

"What do you want?" she asked, opening the door. It didn't help that he looked fantastic, as usual. Jasmine always laughed about Mark's sense of style, which she called "neo-grunge," but what it really amounted to was Mark's complete lack of interest in his appearance. He really had no idea that his ragged, baby-blue polo shirt made his eyes seem even bluer than they were, and that his faded khakis made even his milky arms look tan.

Mark also looked apologetic, which went a long way toward calming Kiki down. But not all the way—oh no. No one who had known Kiki as long as Mark had, had any right to say the things he had said earlier, much less scream them in the middle of school for everyone to hear.

"I wanted to apologize for earlier," he mumbled, staring at his shoes. "That was way out of line."

"No kidding."

"Yeah." He toed a pebble off the top step. "I was all freaked out about Dr. Eckhart, and then you said that thing about the cow's heart." He finally looked up. "Is it true?"

"Would I make up something like that?" She tugged on a dreadlock in frustration. The cow heart had grossed her out, and scared her, too, when she ripped open the pretty, red-wrapped box by the mailbox on Valentine's Day. Her parents made her report it to the police and everything, though they cautioned her not to talk about it, because if whoever sent it knew it had made an impression, they might be tempted to try something even crazier. But it only happened once, and she had never received any sort of threats afterward. She had almost forgotten the whole thing, until the weird incident at school that morning. "Why would I say something like that if it wasn't true? Come on, Mark—you *know* me."

"I thought I did. I don't know. I guess . . . things have changed, you know. Since before the band."

Suddenly Kiki's heart was slamming against her ribs with no kind of rhythm.

"Yeah. A lot of things have changed since we were thirteen."

Was he blushing? Yes, definitely blushing. But was it a good blush, or a bad blush?

He cleared his throat. "Not everything, though. Still best friends?"

He held up a fist that might have been a little shaky. Kiki made a fist and bumped his knuckles gently. Whatever he was really thinking or feeling, he wasn't going to say it. Not yet.

"Of course we are, stupid," Kiki said. "Let's go over to Franklin's."

Franklin's mother, Jade, let them in, but she told them that Franklin was gone.

"Gone where?" Kiki asked Jade's back as she and Mark followed her through the house. It was a gorgeous home, but it could not have been more different from Kiki's. Kiki's house was crammed with her mother's books, prints by the Harlem Renaissance photographer James Van Der Zee, and her father's collection of African tribal masks. Her own room was probably the least cluttered, except for the living room, on a good day. Even the bathrooms were packed with old issues of

Neurosurgery Today that had been crowded out of her father's office, and battered paperbacks by Toni Morrison and Alice Walker that Kiki's mom liked to reread in the tub.

Franklin's house was the complete opposite. There were no bookshelves, no framed photos of Franklin growing up, not even the warm tones of old leather couches with cozy throws for taking naps. Everything in Franklin's house was white. There were white walls, white carpets, white sofas. The first time she came inside, Kiki wondered how a place like that survived Franklin, who spilled sodas on absolutely everything at school except himself. She soon discovered that when Franklin was home he stayed in his bedroom, in the music room, or in the kitchen.

Jade didn't answer Kiki at first, possibly because her arm full of bangles and her belled anklets made so much noise that normal conversation was basically impossible until she sat down, which she finally did, in the kitchen. Jade always dressed in black, and dyed her long hair a flat shade of black even darker than Kiki's.

"Well, I'm not sure where Franklin went," she began, sipping from a chipped coffee cup that had a faded image of a young Michael Jackson on it, back when he had an afro. "Diet Coke?"

"No thanks," Mark and Kiki answered together. Jade lived on Diet Cokes. She was so thin it scared Kiki a little, though Franklin said she had been like that his whole life. Jade had fronted a band herself a long time ago, married a music producer in LA and wound up in Nashville. Jade had expected Nashville to kill her—she'd told Kiki and Mark all about her early fears during the summer tour, more than once. It never seemed to occur to her that Kiki and Mark were from Nashville, and liked it. Jade had thought moving here was the end of the universe, until she actually got to know the city.

"Did you know that Michael Jackson has recorded here in Nashville?" Jade mused, returning to her favorite subject. "Say what you will about the man's private life, but *Thriller* was one fine album. The Jackson Five was good, too. *Everyone* has recorded here—the Beatles, Ray Charles. Did you know that Hendrix got his start playing in the blues clubs north of town, back when he was still in the army?"

Of course Kiki and Mark knew all this perfectly well. Both of them had been born well within Nashville's city limits. But they always listened patiently to Jade's lectures, since they didn't have much of a choice about it either way.

"Yes, we've heard about Hendrix. Do you have any idea where Franklin went?" Mark asked. "We're supposed to be in the studio on Saturday afternoon to record 'Every Angel' for that soundtrack, and we really haven't arranged anything but the melody line."

"I think he said something about a party. I don't know. Is somebody having a party?"

Kiki glanced at Mark, who just shook his head slightly. They knew of at least three Monday-night-football parties starting right after school, but if that's where Franklin went, he would be in no shape for rehearsing by the time they kidnapped him and brought him back home.

"I don't know, Jade. Probably. I guess we'll see you tomorrow," Kiki said.

"Yeah," she answered, and took another sip of her drink. Kiki was not convinced that it was just diet soda. But Jade was a weird woman regardless—she seemed unable to focus on anything but the music business, and she focused on that with the same intensity Kiki saw in her own father when he was examining brain-tissue slides. If it weren't for Jade, they definitely wouldn't have a deal with RGB Records. Unlike Franklin, who cared about Temporary Insanity but cared more about having fun, Jade didn't care about anything but the business side of the band, and Kiki knew they owed their success to her obsession.

"So what do you want to do?" Mark asked on the way back to his car. The sun was already setting, though it was just past five o'clock.

"Get dinner, I guess."

"Loveless Café? Come on, it's great!" he promised when she groaned. The Loveless Café made the must-see list of every tourist who hit the city, but Kiki had never gone. Her parents were from New York, and their idea of comfort food was greasy pizza or take-out lo mein, not hash brown casserole and red-eye gravy. And by the time Kiki was old enough to go out without them she had become a vegetarian, and she had heard rumors that the Loveless put lard in everything.

"I've heard that even the biscuits aren't vegetarian!"

"Biscuits don't eat meat, Kiki."

It was an old argument, and they both laughed on cue. Mark had been making fun of her vegetarianism since the day she stopped eating meat two years ago, on the way to a show in Athens, Georgia. They had stopped at a little country store so Jade could get some more Diet Coke, and Kiki had wandered around back, wondering if they had an outhouse—it was her first visit to a really small town. The little towns outside of

Nashville were more like suburbs, and when they visited other cities, Kiki's family always flew. She thought that the town, called Butler's Grove, was cute.

There wasn't an outhouse in the back, but there was a chicken coop full of silky white hens and little yellow chicks. They all rushed up to Kiki, hoping she was there to feed them. She didn't have any food, obviously, but she managed to pick up one of the chicks anyway. It was the softest, fluffiest thing she had ever held. She had not eaten a single McNugget since that day, or a burger either. This was tough on the road, when Mark and Franklin inhaled every cheeseburger they could find, but Kiki was as stubborn about her vegetarianism as she was about everything else.

"How about Waffle Hut?" Kiki suggested.

"As the lady commands." They both got in Mark's car and shut the doors gently, so that they didn't fall off, and bounced on non-existent shocks all the way to Waffle Hut, their favorite twenty-four-hour diner. There were locations all over the Southeast, but none in nice suburban neighborhoods like Franklin's, so they went to "their" Waffle Hut, in the heart of downtown.

Early in the evening the restaurant was always deserted, though it was a madhouse after 3:00 AM, when the clubs closed. The waitresses were always glad to see Kiki and Mark, because they had never skipped out on a check and were more than generous with their tips. Since a full dinner came to no more than five dollars, it was easy to add a little more than twenty percent, even on Mark's budget. Of course, he now had more than one hundred thousand dollars in the bank from RGB, but his parents wouldn't let him spend a penny until after college.

They split a plate of hash browns drowning in cheese and

fried onions, and joked about the terrible country songs playing on the radio in the restaurant's kitchen. It was, Kiki thought, as if that morning had never happened. But that wasn't quite true. Everything was a little too intense—funny stories funnier, the lights a little too bright. It was almost like being drunk, or wired from too little sleep. There was something a bit different, and not just the relief she felt because she and Mark were not fighting anymore.

"So I said, 'Franklin, A&R stands for Artists and Repertoire, not Arts and Recreation. He's supposed to represent us to the label, not plan our vacations!'"

"Oh my God!" Kiki almost slid out of the booth, she was laughing so hard. "Bill's been our A&R guy for three years! What was he thinking?"

"Bill? He was probably thinking that Franklin does too many drugs."

"You know I meant Franklin," she said, laughing. "He can't possibly be as dumb as he acts. He can really play the guitar, for one thing, and that has to take some brains."

Mark snorted. "It doesn't take that much. You remember the lead singer of the Darlings? Leela, or Lulu, or whatever?"

"Oh, Layla! She was amazing!" Before RGB had assembled the Darlings, Kiki, Mark, and the pianist from another RGB group had backed Layla up on a few showcase pieces. The Darlings had more or less imploded within a year of signing, and Layla was still in rehab, but Kiki had loved working with her.

He shook his head in astonishment. "She is about the best stupid guitarist on the planet."

"How would you know how smart she is?" Kiki teased. She

knew his dating history as well as her own, and she knew that while Layla was in Nashville laying tracks, Mark was half-heartedly going out with a girl from his parents' church. His parents seemed to think that the girl would keep him from doing anything too terrible with his friends in the music scene. In the end, Kiki thought that Mark had corrupted Sarah Jane a little. Not much, because he was about as conservative as a teenaged punk could be, but Kiki was pretty sure that Sarah Jane didn't paint her nails black before she went out with Mark. The last time she saw Sarah Jane, three months after the breakup, she was standing in line at the Exit/In, touching up her manicure with a black Sharpie.

"I have my ways." Mark's eyes sparkled like a swimming pool at night, one of the old-fashioned baby blue ones. There was something about the way the light danced in his eyes, streaks of blue and black. Sometimes his eyes distracted her so badly she forgot to talk. But not this night. Oh, no. She had a feeling that if it was ever going to happen, it would happen tonight.

"No, really!"

"Well, we were stuck at the studio one night, redoing the strings for, oh, I don't know, some song, and we were playing Scrabble between takes. Layla never used a word with more than three letters."

"Come on! Maybe she had really bad letters."

He pointed a fork at her and said, "Kiki Kelvin, anybody who uses the word 'cat' in Scrabble needs to go back to school."

"Remember when Franklin discovered Boggle, and we had to play all the way from Chattanooga to Orlando?"

He laughed so hard he knocked over his coffee cup, and was

still laughing as he apologized to their waitress, Junie, while she mopped it up.

They wrote a little song about Franklin on a Waffle Hut napkin, one they felt sure RGB would never let them record. The alarm on Kiki's cell phone beeped while they worked on the break, reminding them that her curfew was thirty minutes away.

"Okay. Let's roll." Mark was, of course, used to Kiki's parents' rules.

The ride back to Kiki's was quiet—all the giggles had somehow dissolved into a silent tension. Kiki knew that Mark was gearing up to ask her something. She recognized all the usual signs: the way he fidgeted with his left hand, tugging on his too-long hair. She could tell by the way his face went still, like someone with lockjaw.

She thought he was going to let the moment pass when they pulled up in front of her house. Every light was blazing—Kiki's parents always waited up on school nights—but she couldn't see her father's silhouette projected on the curtains in his office or the living room.

"Well, it's been fun," she said. She unbuckled her seatbelt with the speed of a slow-moving glacier, then fidgeted with the lock, giving Mark as much time as she possibly could.

"Um, yeah." He drummed the steering wheel with his left hand. "I've got a question."

"What?" Kiki was amazed that her voice didn't break, but she thought she sounded pretty cool. Better than Mark, who was practically stuttering, staring out the window at her mailbox instead of at her.

"I was wondering . . . is . . . uh . . . is Jasmine seeing anyone?"

Kiki's jaw dropped. If she'd been capable of thought, she would have been glad that Mark wasn't looking at her, but her brain was frozen. After a pause that might have lasted forever, she said, very calmly, "No, she isn't. Should I tell her to expect a call?"

Mark slowly turned to look at her. His face was oddly still. "You don't have to do that."

"I don't mind." She managed a smile, but she didn't think it was very convincing, so she scrambled out of the car at top speed.

"I'll put in a good word for you," she said, then slammed the car door hard enough to rattle every window. She raced up the walk and let herself into the house so fast that anyone watching her would have thought she was being chased. She ran upstairs to her bedroom and slammed that door too. Kicking off her shoes, she wriggled her cell phone out of her back pocket, then collapsed onto her bed.

"Hey, Sash," she said as soon her call connected. Kiki's heart was banging against her ribs arhythmically again. "I think I'm ready to try boy shopping."

The next day after school, Camille, Jasmine, and Sasha went to Kiki's house to go online and browse the available boys.

"What are the ground rules?" Sasha asked, setting up Kiki's account.

"No one younger than me." Kiki was sprawled across her bed, trying to finish a physics problem set she had meant to do the night before, but after she'd got off the phone with Sasha she had cried in the shower for thirty minutes and gone to bed. Even now she wasn't making a lot of progress. Any other day she would have just called Mark for help, but she had had a hard enough time dealing with him face-to-face all day at school. She would rather figure out the relative change in velocity of x on her own than talk to him again.

"Well, obviously you don't want to date a freshman," Sasha said, "but would a sophomore be so bad? I'm putting sixteen and up."

Jasmine and Camille were squeezed into Kiki's one arm-chair, supervising Sasha at the computer. "Young guys aren't the scary part of online dating," Jasmine commented.

"Oh my God, this questionnaire is *endless*," Camille said, amazed. "Kiki, what do you think are the three most important things you're looking for in a guy?"

"Not Mark, not Mark, and not Mark." Kiki erased half of the equation she thought she had just solved, then started over.

"You sure about that?" Jasmine said doubtfully.

"Sure I'm sure. I'm one hundred percent over him," Kiki lied. "Anyway, he wants to ask you out."

"I still think he was kidding," Jasmine said, shaking her head wearily. "He knows I think he has the testicles of an earthworm."

Sasha rolled her eyes. "I think we can safely say that Mark isn't looking for love online anyway," she said, typing away.

"What are you writing? I haven't decided what's most important yet." Kiki put down her graphing calculator and sat up on her bed.

"We're your best friends, except for a certain idiot whose name we're not going to mention," Camille said. "We know what you need."

"What do I need?"

"Someone fun, who can help you forget Mark," Camille replied. Her answer was total Camille: she thought dating was all about having fun.

"Someone sexy," Jasmine said, also typical.

They looked at Sasha, who was chewing thoughtfully on a few strands of purple hair. "Someone clever," she said after a minute. Jasmine gave Sasha a withering look, but Sasha just shrugged. "Hot boys are everywhere. Kiki needs someone who can help her with science homework."

Kiki shoved her books aside and joined the girls at the computer. "I'll figure the homework out on my own, sooner or later. But you're right, I've already got enough stupid boys in my life, and it's not like they're going anywhere."

"Good point. You want someone who is smart enough to surprise you, make you laugh, keep you interested."

"Like Thomas?" Kiki, Jasmine, and Camille chimed together in a syrupy sing-song.

Sasha blushed. "He's pretty sharp, I have to admit. Not to change the subject or anything, but what about your personal statement and photo? I've put in all the favorite subject, favorite hobbies, favorite book stuff, but how would you sum up your view of the world in one hundred words or less?"

That stumped Kiki. "I don't know. What did you put for yours?"

"A poem by Mary Oliver."

"Who?" Camille asked.

"Just a poet. She writes about love and nature and death."

"Your profile was a poem about love, nature, and death?" Jasmine asked disbelievingly. "I'm guessing you got a lot of e-mails, huh?"

"I didn't post my profile, Jazz," Sasha explained. "It was hidden. I just did the compatibility search and sent an e-mail to the three boys who looked interesting. That let them see my profile. All three of them wrote back, I went on two bad dates, and then I met Thomas. That was that."

"What does his profile look like?" Kiki asked.

"A lot like mine, except his poem is by Langston Hughes."

Jasmine shook her head in amazement. "Love poetry? What century do you people live in?"

"Stop it, Jazz. I think it's totally romantic," Camille said dreamily, almost swooning, dark-gold hair swaying over the back of her chair. She looked like someone who belonged on the cover of a romance novel, despite her faded gray Sonic Youth T-shirt.

"You would," Jasmine told her darkly.

"I think my personal statement should be song lyrics," Kiki decided, trading her science notebook for the journal she used for writing.

"How about that Rolling Stones song, 'I Can't Get No Satisfaction'?" Jasmine suggested, her eyes wide with fake innocence.

"Ha ha. I meant some of my own lyrics."

"You want them to know right off that you're *that* Katrina Kelvin?" Sasha asked her seriously.

"I have to post a picture, don't I? They'll know who I am right off." When Temporary Insanity's debut album came out, their pictures were plastered all over Nashville, most prominently in front of the Tower Records store on West End, one of the city's busiest streets. People who had no idea what Temporary Insanity sounded like or what Kiki's name was could recognize her face instantly.

"Well, yeah. But you weren't going to use a publicity shot, were you?"

"I hadn't thought that far," Kiki admitted. But now that Sasha had mentioned it, she could see why that might be a bad thing. She wanted to date someone who was interested in her, not someone interested in dating a girl with a recording contract.

"How about that picture of you getting into the limo before Sophomore Soirée?" Camille suggested. "You looked so pretty in that old ball gown!"

"You looked like Marie Antoinette in blackface and a dreadlock wig," Jasmine countered. "I think you want something a little sexier. How about the one I took when we were at the beach last year for spring break?"

"The one in my bikini? I don't think so." Kiki could just imagine what her managers would have to say if that picture turned up on the Internet.

"How about this one?" Camille suggested, grabbing a framed photo that hung above Kiki's computer. In it, Kiki was dressed for the stage in skintight black pin-striped pants and her favorite black bustier, but she wasn't rocking out. She was lying on a sofa, barefoot, reading *Crime and Punishment* for school. Mark had snapped it with her camera just a few weeks ago.

"Perfect," Sasha said. While Camille slid the photo out of the frame and onto Kiki's scanner, Sasha asked her about her personal statement.

"I don't know," Kiki said, flipping through three years of song lyrics. All of them revealed part of her personality, but no single song summed up everything that it meant to be Kiki Kelvin. "How am I supposed to explain who I am in one hundred words?"

"It's not about who you are," Sasha reminded her. "It's about what you're looking for."

"Huh." Kiki's fingers drifted back through the yellowing pages of her journal. It had traveled with her as far north as Montreal and as far south as Miami Beach, to LA and to DC There were only a few blank pages left, and the cover looked like it had been attacked by mice, but Kiki would miss it when she finally finished the five hundredth page.

"Ready?" she asked Sasha, then she read the lyrics to an unfinished song she had started almost a year ago, on Halloween.

You watch me try on mask after mask
Always knowing which face is true
But when you wonder, you just ask
And that's why I love you.
You always seek beneath the surface
Never frightened of the dark
You understand that I'm an actress
But loving you is not a part
You accept my secrets like a gift
A magic spell only you can lift.

"Isn't that kind of intense?" Jasmine asked. "I mean, you're looking for a boy toy to take your mind off Mark, not your soul mate."

"Kiki is intense," Sasha said. "She doesn't need a guy who can't deal with that."

"Did you write that about Mark?" Camille asked. Her wide-eyed look really was innocent—she had no idea how much it hurt Kiki to be reminded of how wrong she had been about him. Sasha and Jasmine gave Camille dirty looks, but she was oblivious to their stares.

"I thought I did," Kiki admitted. "Are we done? 'Cause I'm ready to move on," she told Sasha firmly.

Sasha grinned and hit "enter."

Faster than Kiki thought possible, four photos popped up, along with names, ages and hobbies. Sasha clicked the first thumbnail, and his profile expanded to fill the screen. Of course, a lot of that was his picture; whoever designed the website made sure that the users had a huge, high-resolution image to check out before the first e-mail was sent.

1. Lyman
Age: 17
Hobbies: percussion instruments, turntables, knitting
Compatibility: 96%
Personal Statement:
> *Carpe diem. Carpe noctem.* You never know how long you have, or what you'll miss out on, so you have to pursue all that's great about being alive. You can't listen to one type of music, or read one type of book, or only eat fruits that grow within twenty miles of your home. Life is too short for that. So seize the day and the night.

"Pretty interesting," Kiki said.

"If by 'interesting,' you mean 'hot.'" Jasmine sighed.

"I meant his personal statement." Lyman seemed like the kind of guy who noticed things, and appreciated what he had. Kiki liked that.

"But, um, dude, look at him. He's hot."

"I didn't say he wasn't." Lyman had lots of curly black hair with eyes to match, and a sharp, foxy face.

"But he's a knitter," Camille said. "No wonder he's single."

"That's a joke," Kiki insisted. "At least, I hope it is. What's behind door number two?"

2. Jacob
Age: 17
Hobbies: electronic music, clubbing, karate
Compatibility: 95%
Personal Statement:
   I am part of the beat
   I am the dark and the heat
   The pulse in your wrist
   The dance in your feet
   A shot of musical whiskey
   Served up neat

"Oh, my God!" The four of them shouted together when Jacob's picture loaded.

"That's really him, isn't it?" Kiki said, peering over Sasha's shoulder at a beautiful brown face staring intensely at the camera. "That's Jacob Young!"

"That's totally him," Sasha said, squinting at the screen. "In all his movie-star glory."

There was a rumor going around Wentworth that Jacob, one of the silent, moody rapper types, was an extra in *Hustle and Flow*. Everyone knew that Jacob's father had produced more than a few rap videos, so maybe he did know Terrence Howard. But no one had ever asked Jacob about it, because no one ever asked Jacob anything. He was so cool, he didn't have to talk to anybody, so he didn't. He wore sunglasses to class every day, even though that was clearly banned in the Wentworth dress code, and not one of their teachers had ever called him on it.

"He's ninety-five percent like you," Sasha said. "I had no idea you two had so much in common."

"I had no idea he was a Temporary Insanity fan. Actually, I thought he thought we were kind of stupid." Of course, he had never said so, but Kiki saw him staring at her now and then from behind his dark glasses, and she had never once caught him smiling.

"Temporary Insanity isn't really electronica."

"Not at all!" Kiki liked electronica well enough, but it was no genre for a drummer. It was all about drum machines. "But his personal statement comes from 'Welcome to the Dance Floor.'"

"Isn't that one of the ones that you wrote?" Sasha asked.

Kiki just blushed.

"He must be your soul mate!" Camille squeaked.

"I don't know," Kiki admitted. "He's awfully quiet. It would weird me out to be with a quiet guy." On the other hand, he had to be a big Temporary Insanity fan to know the lyrics to "Welcome to the Dance Floor." They performed it often, but they had never recorded it, and never posted the lyrics anywhere.

"You can just sit there in silence and look at him," Jasmine said, patting her on the shoulder. "That's a lot more interesting than talking to most guys."

"Point," Kiki admitted. "Door number three?"

Boy Shopping

3. Joshua
Age: 16
Hobbies: lacrosse, lacrosse, and lacrosse
Compatibility: 77%
Personal Statement:

> If you aren't playing to win, you aren't playing. There is
> no problem that's too hard to solve, not on a math
> test, not on a lacrosse field, and not in the community.
> You can sit around complaining about world hunger, or
> you can feed people. Confucius say: Do or do not.
> There is no try. Or maybe that was Yoda. :)

"What do we think, ladies?" Sasha asked.

"I think lacrosse guys have amazing legs," Jasmine said.

Kiki chewed a dreadlock thoughtfully, then asked, "Is lacrosse
the one with big sticks?"

"If you're lucky." Jasmine grinned.

"Jazz, you've got one hell of a filthy mind," Sasha said,
shaking her head. "Kiki, yes, lacrosse is the sport with the big
sticks. The ones with nets on the end."

"I don't know. I don't think jocks are really my type."

"But he can't be one-hundred-percent jock—look at that
personal statement," Camille said. "Real jocks don't even know
who Confucius was."

"I don't know, Cam. He is Asian, and Confucius was an
important Asian spiritual leader," Kiki said.

"He also mentions math tests, and a real jock wouldn't know
what one of those was either," Sasha argued.

"I don't see what the big deal is, Kiki. Look at him." Jasmine was practically bouncing in her seat. Joshua's photo was
clearly snapped in the middle of a game: it only showed his

head and shoulders, but the shoulders in question were very, very broad, and he had a wild grin that promised good times. "Does it matter if he can string two sentences together?"

"Um, actually, yes. I want a real relationship, not just sex."

Jasmine raised her eyebrows, but she didn't say anything.

"You know, I'm not the only one who could use a hot date," Kiki said. "You've been single too long, Jazz. All you think about is getting laid. Sasha, go to number four."

4. Michael
Age: 16
Hobbies: soccer, *Winning Eleven*, making friends, partying
Compatibility: 62%
Personal Statement:
    Why sit around writing personal statements when
    someone somewhere is throwing a party?

"He sounds like fun," Camille said.

"He sounds like an idiot." Kiki sighed and flopped hopelessly back on her bed.

"But look at that picture!"

Kiki had to agree that Michael's looks might make up for the silly personal statement. His skin was the color of sweet iced tea, his eyes were green as dragonflies, and he had a smile that made even Kiki want to sit in his lap.

"He's like catnip to girls, I bet," Sasha said, settling back in her chair.

"But all he wants to do is have fun!"

Jasmine and Camille both looked at Kiki and shook their heads sadly.

"Sweetheart, that's a *good* thing," Camille said. "Mark is Mr. Serious, and look how that turned out."

"Seriously," Sasha added, "Michael might be exactly what you need."

Kiki got Sasha to scroll through all four boys again. Each had his good points and his bad points.

"I just don't know who to choose!"

Jasmine rolled her eyes. "It's just like shopping, dude. You pick something, try it on, and then you decide whether you like it."

"Okay." Kiki looked at the pictures and reread each personal statement. "I've made my decision."

DOES KIKI CHOOSE LYMAN?
Turn to page 59.

❤

DOES KIKI CHOOSE JACOB?
Turn to page 121.

❤

DOES KIKI CHOOSE JOSHUA?
Turn to page 159.

❤

DOES KIKI CHOOSE MICHAEL?
Turn to page 197.

* Chapter 4 *

Lyman

K iki couldn't help squealing when she saw Lyman's e-mail. She had spent forty minutes composing a two-paragraph e-mail introducing herself to him—with the help of her three lovely assistants. Now, less than twelve hours later, came his reply. Fortunately it was 6:53 on Wednesday morning, and Jasmine, Camille, and Sasha were dragging themselves out of their own beds at home, well out of earshot. Kiki didn't want them to know she was the kind of girl who squealed.

From: *lieman@southweb.net*
To: *k^3@rgb.com*
Re: salutations

My dear K-cubed,

After reading your profile and seeing your photo, I'm certain I can safely conclude that your last name is Kelvin. I saw you when you opened for Goodness at the Ryman last month, and at various other clubs at various points in the last few years. I believe you smiled at me two and a half years ago at the End, but I might be mistaken. It was very late, and I think the spotlight was in your eyes.

In response to your question, I don't actually go to school. In theory, my mother is teaching me, but in fact I mostly read books (history, higher math, and graphic novels when I can get away with it) and play the piano. No, I must confess that piano is my percussion instrument of choice, not your beloved drums, but I am pretty good with keyboards. And certainly better than I am with turntables.

I feel I have the advantage, having listened to your music for two years, and you (presumably?) have never listened to mine. The link below will take you to my website, which does have a couple of MP3s, but not a great deal more. Technological know-how is the one area of geekery at which I fail completely.

If you're not ready to run away screaming, give me a call. My number is LOVES-96. This is merely a coincidence that someone else pointed out to me. Really.

—Lyman.

Kiki printed out three copies to take to school, and while her printer spit them out she visited Lyman's website. It was low-key, not a mess of Flash sequences and multiple frames like the Temporary Insanity website that RGB put together. She could already hear her mother down the hall, rattling her car keys ominously, so Kiki just downloaded the three tracks to her iPod without listening first. There would be plenty of time for that during homeroom. She threw on a vintage Black-hearts T-shirt, washed so often it was practically transparent, on top of a lacy black tank top and a pair of skinny jeans.

"Forget you, Mark," she muttered, painting her lips the brilliant red of Hearts Afire.

"Are you ready?" her mother called from downstairs.

"For anything." She threw her copies of Lyman's e-mail into her bag, along with her iPod, and ran for the stairs.

"Dude," Jasmine said in an awed voice, looking up from Lyman's e-mail. It was the first thing anyone had said since Kiki had handed out copies of his letter. She was the only one who had even touched her lunch, even though the break was already half over.

The Pussycat Posse sprawled on the battered sofas of the Senior Common Room, confident that no one would bother them. It was on the fourth floor, and had been a storage room until the student council had it converted for student use. It still smelled like old books, though, and the football field was a better place for hanging out as long as the weather held.

Kiki felt a little silly, working so hard to keep Lyman a secret from everyone but the Pussycats. Mark knew all about Jason Wrightman, and she knew about Sarah Jane, the girl from his parents' church, and everyone else Mark had so much as kissed. But this was different—Kiki had always known that Jason would never replace Mark in her heart. Even though she figured that Lyman would probably be all wrong for her—if he was that great, he wouldn't be looking for love online, right?—she wanted to give it a real shot. And, more impor-tant, Kiki didn't want Mark to think that she was so desperate for a date that she had to find one online, even if it was true.

"What do we think?" Kiki asked, taking another bite of her leftover lo mein.

Jasmine made a horrible face. "We think that Lyman sounds like a freak."

"Speak for yourself, Jazz," Sasha said, folding her copy of Lyman's e-mail into a paper airplane. "I think he sounds cool."

"He sounds *interesting*," Camille corrected her. "But interesting also means weird. What do you think?"

"Well . . ." Everyone paused, waiting for Kiki to say something. The silence went on and on, so Sasha threw her paper airplane at Jasmine, and Jasmine retaliated by throwing some of her microwave popcorn back at her.

"I think he sounds distracting," Kiki announced before the food fight could get out of hand. "And I want to be distracted."

"He sounds like Mark on crack," Jasmine said, ducking behind an armchair. Sasha was pitching ice cubes at her head.

"What are you talking about?" Kiki knew her voice sounded funny, but she couldn't help it. The truth of Jasmine's words hit her like a wave of feedback blasting through stadium speakers.

"He's like Mark two-point-O, the debugged version, with better graphics." Jasmine held up her hands for a truce and Sasha dropped her ice cube back into her soda. "Lyman is smart, like Mark, but even smarter. He's got to be, to write like that. Mark is musical, like Lyman, but Mark only got into it because you and Franklin made him. Lyman is so into it he's competing. And he's got serious talent. Well, you heard him."

"Yeah." All four of them sighed. They had listened to Lyman's music in homeroom on Kiki's iPod. The three tracks from

Lyman's website were pretty amazing. All three began with a piano solo, but they were layered with samples of choirs singing, or a single, scratchy vocal track that had to come from the '20s or '30s, and traffic sounds, and crickets, and all kinds of things that you wouldn't normally think of as music. The production quality was bad enough to give Kiki goosebumps, but the music was phenomenal. No matter what happened between her and Lyman, she was definitely going to get her managers to listen to his demo. His music was a lot better than some of the electronica already in the RGB catalogue.

"I see what you're saying," Camille said. "But there's one important difference between Mark and Lyman."

"Lyman's cuter?" Sasha suggested, sprawling on one of the dusty couches, rejects from the teacher's lounge downstairs.

"Maybe. I think both of them need a haircut." Camille frowned, trying to decide which one was better-looking. Of course, now that Jasmine had mentioned their other similarities, Kiki realized that they even looked a lot alike.

"The big difference between Mark and Lyman is that Lyman actually wants to go out with me," Kiki said, trying not to sound pitiful.

"I already said that Lyman was the smart one," Jasmine said.

"But you also said that he was a freak."

She shrugged. "He is. But I didn't say that was a bad thing."

Kiki sighed, then ate another bite of lo mein. She always meant to wake up early and make herself a real lunch, but she always slept in and wound up eating leftovers.

"Home-school kids are always weird." Jasmine settled next to Kiki on the couch. "But let's face it, K.—you're not exactly the queen of normal."

"I'm not a freak."

"You're a very freaky girl," Jasmine sang in her creaky, atonal alto voice, which always made Kiki laugh. She almost fell off the couch when Jasmine's voice broke on, "The kind you don't bring home to Momma!"

"It's 'mother,' Jazz, and I've never met a mother who didn't like me. They usually think I'm a good influence."

"You usually are a good influence, 'cause you're hanging out with musician types. But you could probably corrupt this Lyman guy, hard-core. I'm telling you, home-school guys are weird little momma's boys." Jasmine paused thoughtfully, then said, "I wonder if he's gay."

Sasha caught Kiki's eyes across the battered coffee table, covered with all that was left of their lunch, and made the "redneck face"—a special combination of lolling tongue and rolling eyes that meant that somebody, usually Jasmine, sounded like a backward and countrified Southerner stereotype.

"Well, I'll let you know if he's gay or not on Saturday morning. We're going out Friday night."

"WHAT?" This time Camille almost fell off the sofa. Kiki didn't know why they were so surprised. She loved her girlfriends, and she always wanted to hear their opinions, but she would never let them tell her who she should go out with.

"We IMed during study hall." The looks on their faces were so funny, Kiki had to bite her tongue to keep from laughing. "What's the big deal? Everybody plays around on computers during study hall."

"They check their e-mail and do research. They don't IM guys they've never met!" Jasmine said severely.

"That's because most people are at school. But I knew he

wouldn't be, so I logged into HelloHello. It said that he was online, so we talked."

"What did you talk about?" Sasha asked.

"Nothing really. How tired I was, how bored he was. I was only online for thirty minutes."

"Did you ask him out?" Jasmine asked.

"He said, 'Busy Friday at seven?' I said, 'No,' and that was that."

Of course, it was a little more complicated than that. Kiki didn't mention that she had IMed him because she was afraid to call him, or that her hands were shaking as she typed. It wasn't just that she was weirded out by this whole boy-shopping thing, though she still thought it was pretty strange. Kiki felt, for reasons she couldn't explain, even to herself, that going out with Lyman meant that she had given up on Mark for real. She didn't know why this was so different from Jason Wrightman, Luke Sheppherd, or any of the other boys she had dated, but somehow it was.

"Don't you have a show?" Jasmine asked.

"We've already headlined the Exit/In and City Hall, and we opened at the Ryman twice this fall. RGB wouldn't book us in a smaller venue here in town. The contract won't let us travel more than one weekend a month, and we're playing three shows in New Orleans Halloween weekend." Kiki had already explained this two hundred times, but Jasmine could never remember their schedule. Kiki couldn't blame her—she had a hard time keeping track of it herself. Even Mark, who had asked his parents for a PalmPilot for his thirteenth birthday, needed all the help he could get.

"So where're you guys going for your first date?" Sasha asked.

"I don't know."

"You haven't decided?" Jasmine asked.

"He won't tell me."

"What?" Camille sounded confused.

"It's a surprise." Kiki wasn't sure how she felt about that. Lyman seemed pretty harmless, but what did she know? He could be a serial killer, planning to drag her into the woods and butcher her. But if he thought she was a pushover because she was a girl, he was in for a surprise. Her parents had forced her to take karate classes before hitting the road for the first time, and she still sparred with her sensei a couple of times a month.

"So what are you going to wear?"

"I don't know. He said to dress up."

"Oooh. Isn't there some sort of costume ball this weekend?" Camille's parents went to every black-tie event Nashville had to offer and were in the paper every other week. Kiki wondered if that had something to do with Camille's hatred of dressing up, but she had never asked.

"I don't think he's taking me to a charity ball for our first date. He didn't say anything about a costume, for one thing, just a dressy dress."

"Well, you've got plenty of those. You'll be fine."

"Of course I will." Kiki tipped the take-out carton and slurped the last few bits of vegetable. "It's just a date."

"Oh, yeah?" Jasmine grinned. "We'll see how you feel on Friday night."

Sasha talked Jasmine and Camille into attending the Wentworth-Carroll football match with her, Thomas, and a couple of his friends after school Friday night, so they never got to see exactly how freaked out Kiki was an hour before Lyman was supposed to pick her up. Both of her parents were home, but they politely pretended not to notice that she was wearing a different outfit every time she marched from their huge master bathroom with its three-way mirror to the spare room where she stored clothes she didn't often wear.

The problem was the phrase "dress up." It could mean anything from church clothes to black tie, and Kiki was not about to ask Lyman what he meant by it. She hadn't contacted him since the quick IM session at school on Wednesday—she didn't want to look too eager. She might not get out much, but she knew that too much interest was a turnoff for every guy she had ever met. She had tried on everything she owned, from the little black dress her mom had bought her for her first dressy party to a full-fledged ball gown she found in New York, and had paid a fortune for. She still had no idea what to wear.

She was staring at three Kikis, all wearing a fragile midnight-blue silk gown from the 1930s, sprinkled with rhinestone stars, when her cell phone sang out, *A friend in need is a friend indeed. A friend who'll tease is better.*

"Hey," she said without checking the number. For everyone except her closest friends, the ring tone was an old Das EFX/Ice Cube song that began, "Check yourself, before you wreck yourself."

"Hey," Mark said, scaring Kiki half out of her skin. She just assumed it was the Pussycats, calling to check up on her. But Mark didn't seem to notice that anything had changed between them. He had driven her to and from practice all week, and they had talked as usual: scheduling the scratch tracks due at

RGB in mid-November, homework, how annoying Franklin was. He hadn't mentioned taking Jasmine out again, and she hadn't breathed a word about Lyman. "What's up?"

"Oh, nothing. What's up with you?" Kiki hoped she didn't sound squeaky. She had a lot of talents, but lying wasn't one of them, and her voice usually climbed half an octave when she was hiding something.

"Nothing much. Thinking about going to that Trip-Hop Triple Threat at the Maze. You going?"

"I don't think so." She almost added, "I've got a date," but she didn't. She was hoping, of course, that he would be jealous. But he was more likely to say, "Congratulations."

"Oh. Okay. Well, I guess I'll see you tomorrow."

"Yeah, sure," she answered, though she wasn't at all sure where she was supposed to see him. Were they scheduled to be in the studio? Or maybe he just assumed that they would run into each other somewhere—Laura Keller's party, maybe? She didn't have time to try to figure it out—Lyman would be there in twenty minutes, and she had just discovered a moth hole in a place where it wouldn't go unnoticed. It would be easy to fix if she had some spare rhinestones lying around, but she didn't.

"Talk to you later, Mark." She hung up and ran back to the spare room. She threw on a silver satin ball skirt that she'd bought because it had pockets, and a silk-knit tank top in basic black. The casual top balanced the formal skirt, making it appropriate for any special occasion—that's what Kiki told herself, anyway. She didn't have the time for another costume change. The doorbell rang as she was carefully lining her lips, jarring her so she drew way outside the lines. She cursed, dabbed on a bit of makeup remover, and started over. She knew that her father would trap Lyman with supposedly friendly small talk for ten minutes anyway.

When she made her way downstairs she could hear Lyman laughing at something her father had said. It was a nice laugh, low but light, and not too loud. It didn't sound forced either, which said something about Lyman. Most of Dr. Kelvin's jokes had to do with cutting into people's brains, which was not a subject most people considered funny. Kiki couldn't decide if it was a good thing or a bad thing that Lyman seemed to be getting along with her father just fine.

"*Here* she is. I told you she wouldn't take long." Kiki thought her father was standing somewhere near the fireplace. She wasn't sure, because the instant she saw Lyman relaxing on the couch, she couldn't look away.

"Maybe he *is* gay," she thought once her brain started working again. He was wearing a simple black suit that fit—really fit, unlike the vast majority of suits Kiki saw on her classmates on Parents' Day at Wentworth. Under it, he wore a fitted, faded purple T-shirt that matched both the lavender rosebud in his lapel buttonhole and the laces in his battered black sneakers. He had a bouquet of purple roses for Kiki, and a brilliant smile. His wild hair was paler in person than it seemed in the picture, and his eyes were more hazel than blue, but, if anything, he looked better in real life. If Jasmine were here, she would definitely pronounce him hotter than a biscuit—even if she would tease him mercilessly about all the purple.

"Hi," Kiki said, hoping she didn't sound as shy as she suddenly felt.

"Salutations!" He leapt to his feet, terrifying the cat, Mr.

Lister, who was curled up at the other end of the couch. Mr. Lister shot toward the kitchen, which gave Kiki's mother an excuse for wandering into the living room herself.

"Oh, a guest! I didn't know you were here. I'm Janine Kelvin." Unlike Kiki, her mother lied smoothly. "Let me put those in some water . . ."

"This is Alex Lyman," Dr. Kelvin supplied on cue.

"Lovely to make your acquaintance, Mrs. Kelvin. And please, call me Lyman."

Kiki looked on in horror as Lyman approached her mother with his hand outstretched. She thought he might actually bow and kiss her hand. She could deal with the ten-dollar words, but if he had eighteenth-century manners, too, no matter how hot he was they were in a lot of trouble. Mark and Franklin would make fun of him twenty-four-seven. Jasmine, too.

Fortunately, when he finally made his way across the room, avoiding the ottomans, occasional tables, and stacks of magazines, he gave Mrs. Kelvin a firm handshake before handing over the bouquet. Handshakes were fine.

"Katrina, come choose a vase," her mother said, and Kiki reluctantly followed her into the kitchen.

"Where on earth did you meet that creature?" her mother asked, pulling a few dusty vases from underneath the sink. "He looks like he's about to start tap dancing or something."

"How about the blue vase?" Kiki suggested, carefully avoiding the question. She wasn't sure how her parents would feel about her going out with a guy she met online.

"It clashes with the flowers."

"I know. But I like it." Kiki drifted toward the door. "You can just leave them on the counter. I'll take them up to my room later."

"Whatever you say, Kiki. Have a nice night."

"Thanks, Mom. Don't wait up."

Kiki thought she heard her mother say, "Yeah, right," but she wasn't sure. Lyman and her father were laughing uproariously again at something her father had said, ending with, "Sure I expected to find it. But not up there!"

"Are you ready to go?" Lyman asked her as she entered the room.

"You bet. See you later, Dad."

"Have a good time."

Kiki paused for a moment, waiting for him to add his habitual threat. She sometimes thought he spent all week thinking them up—some of them were seriously disturbing, even if Mark, Franklin, and even Jason thought he was kidding. But her dad didn't say anything about evisceration, abacination, or any other twisted, medieval methods of torture that Kiki had had to look up in the dictionary.

"Good night, Dr. Kelvin. It was a pleasure meeting you."

Lyman opened the door for Kiki, then followed her down the walk. He helped her into his newish Volvo so politely that Kiki wondered if he thought her parents were watching from the window. Ordinarily they would be, but her mother was probably still in the kitchen, cutting the ends off the rose stems, and Lyman had charmed her father completely. Maybe he thinks Lyman's gay, too, she thought, and she had to stifle a giggle as Lyman let himself into the driver's side.

"So, I'm Lyman, as you probably gathered," he said, clearing his throat twice. His voice slid up and down anyway, the car keys jangling in counterpoint as he cranked the ignition. Kiki could see that he was as nervous now that he was alone with her as he had been comfortable dealing with her parents. This was a very bad sign. The whole point of trying HelloHello was to find boys who weren't intimidated by her. If he couldn't get through five minutes of small talk without blushing crimson, she was in for a long night.

"Yeah, I figured that much out." She watched him wince, and had to stop herself from laughing out loud. This was ridiculous. He had to know how hot he was—there was a mirror in his house somewhere. And he came off as more than a little arrogant in front of her parents. If he didn't pull himself together, this relationship would be over before it began, no matter how cute he was. "But your first name is Alex?"

"Only my mother calls me Alex," Lyman told her. "So I seriously hope you won't."

"Okay, *Lyman*," she said, drawing out his last name for emphasis.

"Your real name is Katrina?" he asked.

"Katrina Isabella Kelvin."

"So 'Kiki' comes from your initials?"

"Nope." She slouched in her seat, not exactly looking forward to spending the evening with someone who asked such boring questions. They were headed toward the interstate, which meant they were going someplace downtown. She crossed her fingers, hoping it would be someplace interesting.

"And Kiki is not usually a diminutive of Katrina," he continued.

"No, it's not. Katrina is a diminutive of Katherine, and it is redundant to truncate a truncation." *You're not the only one who knows a few big words,* she added silently.

"So where'd you get the nickname?"

"Guess."

Oddly, he seemed to perk up at the challenge. His brilliant smile was back, brighter than ever. "Okay, let's see. You're listed as Kiki Kelvin on the liner notes to *Free for All*, so it's not a reaction to Hurricane Katrina."

She shook her head. She didn't like sharing her name with such a terrible storm, but she had already been Kiki to her friends for years when the hurricane flattened the Gulf Coast.

"Big anime fan?"

"When I actually have the time to sit down and watch a movie, yes, but I didn't name myself after *Kiki's Delivery Service*."

"It's great, isn't it? I like it better than *Spirited Away*."

"*Spirited Away* is a much better movie!" Kiki said, straightening up.

"Technically, I'd agree with you. But I like *Kiki's Delivery Service* better. There's something about the tone, I guess you'd say, that's so much lighter—"

Soon they were arguing like she and Mark did on a good day. Lyman wasn't hung up on being right, though—he was as eager to listen to Kiki as to make his own case. And Kiki was so busy defending *Spirited Away*, even if it was a lot more depressing than *Kiki's Delivery Service*, that she didn't realize where they were going until Lyman pulled into a parking lot behind the Schermerhorn Center.

Oh no, she thought, but it was too late to try to convince Lyman to take her somewhere else. Schermerhorn was the just-built home of the Nashville Symphony, a building Kiki had toured with her arts appreciation class in the second week of school. And she did appreciate the building itself—she dreamed of playing a venue with acoustics like the Schermerhorn. But she wasn't crazy about classical music. She only took the class because it seemed like a good way to get more sleep three days a week—she had napped through slide shows on painting, architecture, and sculpture, and snored through two weeks of Bach and Brahms. Any teacher who played nineteenth-century lullabies to teenagers after lunch ought to know what to expect.

But Lyman was still rattling on about Japanese movies, nodding at the ticket-taker by the door as if he knew her by name. Kiki didn't think he was showing off—he really seemed to know the Schermerhorn well. And he seemed completely unaware that Kiki might not be quite as happy about being there as he was.

"Tonight's program is kind of special," he whispered as they took their seats. They were good seats, too—only ten rows back. Kiki had no idea how much symphony tickets cost, but she knew it was a lot more than dinner and a movie. "The guest pianist is one of my teachers, Jascha Kent. He almost never performs now, since he's got arthritis, but he's amazing. He hasn't played on stage in two years."

"Um, wow." There went any chance of convincing him to leave before the concert started, while he could maybe get a refund on the tickets. Well, there was always the off chance that he'd be willing to sneak out during intermission. "How long have you been playing the piano?"

"Basically forever. My mom started teaching me when I was three, I think. She says I wanted to learn, but that's not how I remember it."

"But you must like it now."

"Well, yeah. I love it. But I'm not sure I want to do it professionally. I sometimes feel like . . . oh, I don't know. I mean, I love playing. Really. And I like traveling, too, and the competitions. But sometimes I wish I did something a little more . . . normal, I guess. You know? I haven't gone to a real school since I was eight."

"You're not missing much," Kiki said, but she gave his arm a little squeeze. After all, she knew exactly what he meant.

He smiled, and was about to say something else when the lights went out.

"Welcome to the Schermerhorn Center. Please silence your cell phones," boomed a recorded voice in the darkness, so Kiki and Lyman both whipped theirs out and switched from ring to vibrate. Onstage, lights bloomed, and the curtain opened to reveal the orchestra already in place. The concertmaster—the lead violin—got to her feet and played a clear, ringing "a." Soon, the magnificent acoustics magnified the chaos of an entire orchestra tuning up, but it was silent again after a minute. Kiki knew that the piano was not always part of an orchestra, but she was surprised to see that there was no piano onstage.

"I thought you said your teacher was a pianist," Kiki whispered.

"He's playing in the second half, after intermission."

Oh well. Another plan foiled. Kiki sighed silently and settled in for a couple of hours of sheer boredom. She hadn't decided what she was doing with the beats on a couple of their new songs—if the music wasn't too annoying, maybe she could get that figured out. But if she was going to be sitting quietly for two hours, she would rather get some reading done for AP English. Unfortunately, that was not an option.

The conductor walked onstage, a very tall woman with long,

dark hair, wearing the traditional conductor's tuxedo. The faint buzz of whispered conversations died as she crossed the stage, bowed swiftly, then climbed onto the little dais that held her music stand. She waved a slim ivory wand up once, then down, and the orchestra plunged into something fast and wild that Kiki had never heard before. It sounded more like Latino dance music than Brahms lullabies, but there was a certain sophistication along with the swing. It was fascinating, which was not something Kiki said about a lot of music. Unlike when she listened to rock, this music made her want to dance *and* to think.

"What is this?" Kiki whispered, speaking right into Lyman's ear so that she wouldn't disturb the old people sitting to either side of them.

"Villa-Lobos," he whispered back, handing her the program. "Like it?"

"I love it!"

The woman sitting to Kiki's left shushed her. Kiki just smiled, settled back, and enjoyed the music. She had no idea a symphony could sound like this! At some point, Lyman took her hand, and she saw no reason to snatch it back. His hand was warm and dry; it fit like a puzzle piece. Where his left wrist pressed against her right, she could feel his pulse racing in time with hers.

After three fast pieces with lots of interesting rhythms going on with the tympanis, snare, and bass drums, they played a slow, dreamy piece by another composer Kiki's arts appreciation teacher had never mentioned. Then the lights came up, and Kiki and Lyman joined the line snaking out of the auditorium and into the lobby.

"So, what do you think?" he asked, grinning because he already knew the answer.

"Of course it was awesome. Hey, where are we going?" Kiki asked as Lyman led her to an unmarked door near the end of the lobby.

"I told Jascha that we'd come backstage and say hello."

"Don't you think someone will stop us?" she whispered as they slipped through the door into a narrow hall. There were a couple of security guards at the other end of the hall.

He winked at her and led the way. If he hadn't been holding her hand, Kiki probably would have snuck back out. She knew that security guards might look like cops who've had a few too many doughnuts, but most of them took their work pretty seriously. One of the roadies on the Wasted tour was shot in the foot when he refused to tell a guard who he was and didn't produce his ID badge fast enough.

"Alex Lyman to see Jascha Kent," Lyman announced when they were halfway down the hall.

"Who did you say you are?" asked one of the guards.

"Alex Lyman. I played with Youth Symphony last month."

The younger guard nodded slowly. "Oh, yeah, I remember seeing you around. You're here to see who?"

"Jascha Kent, the soloist."

The guards looked at each other, shrugged, and got out of the way. Kiki was impressed: Lyman seemed totally confident in this world.

The area backstage wasn't that different from any venue Kiki had visited: musicians stood around drinking bottled water and gossiping. It took less than a minute for Lyman to find

Jascha—he was sitting on a stool in a corner, wiggling his fingers in some kind of warm-up exercise.

"Lyman!"

"Mr. Kent!" They didn't shake hands or hug, like Kiki expected, but she could tell they were happy to see each other. Interesting. She couldn't imagine any of the Pussycat Posse eager to see a teacher outside of school.

"This is Kiki Kelvin," Lyman said, tugging her forward.

"You look familiar. Was your face outside of Tower Records a few months back?"

"More like a year, but yeah. Nice to meet you."

Jascha Kent wasn't as old as Kiki thought—his brown hair was only sprinkled with silver. But when he stood up, he moved very slowly—you could tell he expected pain. A career in classical music was so precarious—anything from arthritis to earaches could mean a forced early retirement. Rock was, if anything, worse: the touring schedule was hard on the body, there was the constant temptation of heavy drugs, or alcohol at least, and who wants to watch a middle-aged woman rock out? Probably the average age for a drummer was twenty-five, and Kiki knew fewer than ten who were over thirty.

Jascha asked them what they thought about the first half of the program, and Kiki told him how much she liked newer symphonic music.

"You'll probably like the Rachmaninoff then. At least, I hope you will." He smiled at her, a young man's smile, then hustled them back to the side door. They had to jog down the hall to get back into the auditorium before the doors shut, and then apologize to half a dozen people as they crawled over their laps, back to their seats. When the curtain came up, Kiki joined the crowd applauding Jascha's triumphant, if slow, walk across the stage.

"This is going to be great," Lyman whispered, and it was. The Rachmaninoff piece sounded older than the Villa-Lobos— or, at least, it wasn't from the new world. But it was wild, fast, and complicated, and Kiki gripped Lyman's hand the whole time, except when the audience broke into applause. At the very end, a choir joined the orchestra onstage, and they performed part of *Carmina Burana*. Kiki actually was familiar with that piece, from movie trailers and dramatic Superbowl commercials, as well as from arts appreciation. But she had never heard it performed live—it was a completely different experience. The jumps that seemed melodramatic on recordings were strangely moving in live performance. She sighed and rested her head on Lyman's shoulder, close to tears.

At the end of the concert, the audience responded with thunderous applause, Kiki clapping as loudly as everyone around her.

"That was amazing!" Kiki was almost dancing in the aisles as they made their way to the exit. The old woman who had shushed her earlier smiled and said to her equally old husband, or maybe date, "It's so nice to see young people appreciating real music, not that punk rock stuff."

They laughed, and Lyman's arm somehow found itself around Kiki's shoulders. For a guy who didn't seem to spend a lot of time around girls, Lyman could be pretty slick. He even smelled delicious—Kiki had been appreciating his cologne since he first whispered in her ear.

She enjoyed it even more once they stepped outside of the Schermerhorn. A frosty wind was blowing off the river, belling

Kiki's skirt and freezing her bare arms. Lyman slipped his jacket around her shoulders before she even had time to complain of the cold.

"I should have brought a wrap at least," she said, snuggling into the crook of his arm. "I didn't think it would get cold so fast."

"But you've got such nice shoulders." He sounded completely serious. Kiki got her share of compliments, of course, but she didn't think anyone had ever told her that she had nice shoulders.

"Long gloves, then," she said. "But I don't suppose they'd be warm enough."

"Depends on what they're made of. There's a really nice synthetic silver yarn at Threaded Bliss. You could stripe that with black cashmere, and that would make them warm. If you made them ribbed and fingerless, you could probably knit them up in just a few hours."

Kiki stopped dead to look up at Lyman's face.

"What?" he asked, eyebrows innocently raised.

"Oh my God." This time, Kiki couldn't hold back the giggles. "You really do knit!"

"What can I say? I've got a lot of free time."

"But why?"

"Why not? I'm supposed to break my leg playing football, or lose a few brain cells playing *Warcraft*, just because I was born with a Y chromosome? I'm not going to let other people's ideas of what guys do determine what I do with my free time."

"Well, okay. I can see that."

"A female drummer in a hard-core band? I bet you can."

Kiki was saved from coming up with a response by the buzz of a vibrating phone.

"I'm guessing this is for you," she said, fishing his phone out of his jacket pocket. She glanced at the screen and did a double-take. The first half of the number displayed was Jasmine's, the second half, Camille's. *If their cell phones had a baby*, she thought, stifling a giggle, *that would be its number!* She handed the phone to Lyman.

He checked the number then slipped the phone into his pants pocket.

"Anyone special?"

"Not really. Are you hungry?"

"Starving." She was too nervous to eat before the show, but now she could kill a plate of hash browns.

"Are you a vegan or just a vegetarian?"

"Just vegetarian."

"How do you feel about Waffle Hut? There's one right around the corner, near the clubs, and they do a killer grilled cheese sandwich."

"Know it well." Kiki smiled. "Perfect."

Because of the cold, Lyman and Kiki had the sidewalk to themselves, though Broadway was clogged with cars, which was to be expected on a Friday night. It was quiet enough that Kiki could hear Lyman's cell phone buzzing in his pocket four times before they got to Waffle Hut.

"You're a popular guy, huh?" Kiki asked as he held the door open for her.

"You have no idea." He grinned. Kiki smiled back—she'd had nights on the road when the Pussycat Posse had filled the entire missed-call queue on her cell phone. If she hadn't specifically warned them not to call her that night, she knew that each one of them would have called to check up on her at least once.

They slid into a booth, and a few minutes later two grilled cheese sandwiches were frying in a puddle of what passed for butter at Waffle Hut.

"You can order meat," Kiki had told him. "I don't mind."

"I've been a vegetarian since I was nine," he said.

"What happened when you were nine?"

"I saw *Babe*."

"Huh."

"What?"

"I was just thinking . . . you watch a lot of movies."

He shrugged. "Not going to school gives you a lot of free time."

"So what do you do when you aren't watching movies or knitting?"

"Or playing the piano? That does take up a lot of time. Oh, I do workbooks, play around with some of my dad's old recording equipment, read manga and old *Sandman* comics. What about you? What do you do when you're not at school or working on music?"

"That's pretty much all I do, really. I used to read graphic novels—I loved *The Sandman*, and I like Alan Moore's stuff, you know, like—"

Kiki forgot what she was saying when she saw who was walking into Waffle Hut. Jasmine's face was turned away, since she was talking over her shoulder, but Kiki would recognize the particular shade of her hair from half a mile away. And the person she was talking to?

Mark.

"Is something wrong?" Lyman asked, swiveling to look behind him.

"Wrong? No. Of course not." Kiki's heart was banging like a drum-track playback on double speed. She had talked to Mark and Jasmine every single day that week, and neither one mentioned that Mark had asked Jasmine out, much less that she had said yes.

"Are you sure?" Lyman turned back to face Kiki. He held her hands with both of his and peered into her face. She knew she must look absolutely awful for him to be so concerned.

"Yes, I'm sure," Kiki lied, plastering a false smile on her face. Waffle Hut was not a large restaurant. They would see her sooner or later, and if she didn't say anything it would be even worse. She cleared her voice and called, "Jazz! Mark! Hey!"

Jasmine's face, pale to begin with, went stark white. Mark turned pink, but both of them managed to sound perfectly normal when they said hello to Lyman, though Mark's face had gone strangely still. Kiki wasn't quite as successful. She almost introduced Mark as her friend, choked halfway through the word, then said he was the bassist for Temporary Insanity, as if that was all he was to her. Kiki didn't introduce Jasmine at all. She clearly wasn't the friend that Kiki had thought her to be.

"Is something going on with the band?" Lyman asked as soon as Jasmine and Mark settled at the other end of the diner, out of Kiki's line of sight.

"There's always something going on with the band. We're called Temporary Insanity for a reason." She sighed. Of course, she had told Jasmine that she was over Mark. She must have said it one hundred times since Tuesday morning. But she never thought Jasmine would actually go out with him. She didn't really think Mark would have the guts to call her. Other guys were scared of Jasmine—she was kicked off the debate team for being too mean in cross-examination. She actually made a boy from Carroll cry at her first and last tournament.

"I'm sorry to hear that." Lyman gave her hands a gentle squeeze. "I think you're really strong, to handle the pressure as well as you do."

Kiki could feel herself blushing. "Um, thanks. I mean, I don't think I do all that great a job at it really, but—"

"Seriously. I'm on the periphery of the industry myself, remember. You're fantastic."

"Wow. Thanks, Lyman. For the record, I think you're pretty impressive, too." She twined her fingers around his and leaned across the table. She knew Jasmine would think this kiss was for their benefit, and maybe Mark would, too, if he had half a clue. But it really was all about Lyman, his reward for saying just the right thing at just the right time.

Kiki discovered that he didn't spend all of his free time watching movies and knitting. Either someone had taught him how to kiss properly, or he was as naturally gifted at that as he was with the piano. It began with gentle pressure of lips on lips, then tongue on tongue, his stubble just barely stinging her chin; their hands were clasped so tight it almost hurt. With her eyes shut, all the sounds of the diner should have seemed louder than before. Instead, the whole world had disappeared except for Kiki and Lyman, joined by hands and lips and a mutual attraction roaring through their veins. Kiki was glad they were sitting down—she was more than a little dizzy.

"Get a room, kids," said their waitress, slamming down two fresh cups of coffee and two plates of grilled cheese with a side of hash browns, extra pickles for Kiki.

They jumped apart, Kiki's heart beating in her throat, Lyman's eyes gleaming. She took a sip of her coffee, resisting the urge to look over her shoulder at Mark and Jasmine. She might have forgotten about them while she was kissing Lyman, but she remembered now. And she was still so flustered that she forgot to add cream and sugar to her coffee. She swallowed the acrid mouthful with a shudder, which made Lyman laugh.

"I don't know what I was thinking," she murmured, pouring a glittering stream of sugar into her cup. "And how is your dinner?"

Lyman grinned and took a bite of his sandwich.

"Delicious," he said.

Kiki couldn't agree more.

On the way back to Kiki's house, they talked nonstop. Like Kiki, Lyman liked hot weather, southern-fried tofu, and all kinds of music. Unlike Kiki, he also liked game shows, tempeh, and pre-calculus, but Kiki was sure they could work that out, and any other differences they might have. Mostly the website had been right—they were amazingly compatible.

She made him park half a block from her house since her father had binoculars and he wasn't afraid to use them. Not that he would have seen anything too scandalous. Kiki was more or less in Lyman's lap, her fingers plunged in his soft hair, while he kissed his way from her ear to her collarbone. Both of his hands were under her shirt, pressed against her back, bringing her closer to him. Her head was swimming, all thought of her curfew pushed out of mind by the slight, delicious pain of Lyman's teeth on the delicate skin at the base of her throat. But eventually a weird vibration between his left hip and her right knee managed to distract her. His phone vibrated again. And again. And again.

"Are you sure you don't need to answer that?" she asked, pulling back from him.

"What? Oh. No. It's fine."

"What if it's some kind of emergency?"

"It's not an emergency."

"Aren't you even going to check?"

He sighed and fished the phone out of his pocket. He flipped it open, and Kiki saw that every single missed call was from the same number. The half-Jasmine/half-Camille number. It filled the screen, except for the band across the top showing the time. She thought about teasing him about all the calls, but then decided against it. Lyman flipped the phone shut and slipped it back into his pocket.

"You know, I should probably be going," she said, sliding back over to the passenger side to pull her clothes back together. "My curfew is up in seven minutes."

"It can't take more than two minutes to walk to your house from here. That leaves five minutes, six if I drive. And I'd be happy to."

"No thanks. I like to walk."

"Won't you be cold?"

She grinned a wicked grin. "I think I need to cool off. Goodnight." She kissed him again, briefly this time, and scuttled out of the car, leaving his coat inside. He sat there until she had her front door open, then she heard his car starting behind her.

On her way up the stairs, she checked her phone for the first time that night. Three calls in the last hour, all from Jasmine, plus a couple of text messages. Kiki didn't feel up to dealing with her just yet. She wasn't even sure what she thought about the situation. She knew what she felt, all right, but thoughts were different from feelings.

"How was your date?" her father shouted from the master bedroom.

"Fine." And it *was* fine—better than fine, mostly. But there was something not quite right about those missed calls of Lyman's. Franklin and Mark both called Kiki all the time, for work stuff or just to hang out, but they never called more than twice in a row. Lyman would probably think she was being sexist, but calling continuously just wasn't guy-friend behavior. Girls, though—the Pussycat Posse did it all the time, even if there was nothing in particular going on. The only time Kiki could remember a guy calling her constantly was when she dumped James Johnston in the tenth grade. Whether it was some ex who didn't want to be an ex anymore, or a female friend who was really, really curious about how Lyman's date was going, Kiki had a gnawing feeling that it wasn't a good sign.

She almost sent Lyman an e-mail about it, and then erased the message at the last minute. If there really was something going on, he was more likely to lie about it over e-mail than face to face. And if it was no big deal, she would look like an idiot for getting all freaked out about it. This was waaaay too soon to be getting possessive.

"I'll figure it out in the morning," she promised herself as she shimmied out of her clothes. She put on an extra-large Temporary Insanity T-shirt and lay down, too weary to even take off her makeup. Her mother always got mad about lipstick on the pillowcases, but Kiki was so tired, she fell asleep before she remembered to feel bad about it.

✳ Chapter 5 ✳

Version 2.0

Kiki woke up to her mother's grumbling and entirely too much sunlight for a Saturday morning.

"I'm sorry," Kiki muttered, dragging the pillow over her head. "I'll wash my sheets myself. Later."

"I said that you have a guest, young lady."

"What? I can't have a guest. What time is it?"

"Eight-thirty. Now get up. I want to put your pillowcase in the wash before the stain sets."

"Mooooooooom!"

"Get up!"

Kiki knew when she was beaten. She dragged herself out of bed and put on a pair of Jason's Beautiful Youth boxer shorts, then headed downstairs.

"You're up early," she growled when she found Jasmine in the kitchen.

"I texted you I was coming. Here. Venti nonfat sugar-free caramel latte with extra foam." Jasmine slid the giant cup of coffee across the table. "Plus Krispy Kremes in the oven, to keep them hot."

"So not hungry." Kiki accepted the coffee, though, and said, "Thanks. So," she added with as much restraint as possible, "how was your date with Mark?"

Jasmine rolled her eyes. "It wasn't a date. Not a *date* date, anyway. He asked me if I wanted to check out a few trip-hop bands at the Maze; I said yes. He didn't put the moves on me or anything. In fact, I'm kind of wondering how much he really likes girls."

"That is not the point," Kiki hissed, trying to keep her voice down. Her parents stayed out of her problems with the band, but they had no qualms about butting into friend issues. "You know how I felt about him. I never would have believed that you'd go out with him."

"Felt. Past tense. Supposedly." Jasmine sipped her own drink, a nonfat white mocha, extra whip—Kiki knew Jasmine's taste in drinks as well as her taste in men. Or so she thought.

"What about the six-month rule?" Kiki demanded.

"The six-month rule applies to ex-boyfriends, not people you haven't actually dated."

"But still! Jazz, you're supposed to be one of my best friends. You knew I'd be upset. How could I not be upset?"

"Well, I didn't expect you to find out."

Kiki took a deep breath so that when she started screaming she wouldn't have to stop for a long time, but Jasmine cut her off.

"Dude, you know I have no interest in Mark. None. Not now, not ever. I don't even get how you could waste so much time on him in the first place."

"So why did you say yes when he asked you out?"

"'Cause I wanted to find out what he really thought about *you*."

Kiki cocked an eyebrow at her. "And how did that work out?"

Jasmine snorted. "Not too well. Mark's even better at avoiding questions than you are."

"It's all those interviews. We get a lot of practice."

They silently sipped coffee while Kiki considered everything Jasmine had said.

"I guess I believe you," Kiki finally decided. "I mean, you think Mark's an idiot. Right?"

"Pretty much." She grinned. "He is fun to look at, though. I'll give you that."

"Not unlike Mr. Lyman."

"Oh, my God, he's even cuter in person, isn't he?"

"Yep." Kiki fished a doughnut from the box in the oven while Jasmine commented on every aspect of Lyman's appearance, from his shiny hair to the purple laces on his shoes.

"All that purple, though. So very gay."

"He definitely likes girls," Kiki said, rejoining her at the table.

"You know for sure?"

"For sure."

"Oh, my God! Tell me all about it!"

"A lady doesn't kiss and tell, Jazz. We need to find you a guy so you can have some fun on your own."

"A real guy, not your sloppy seconds."

"No kidding."

"So tell me about your date. Not the sex-standing-up-in-the-Waffle-Hut-bathroom part, but the rest of it."

Kiki laughed at the image. She loved Waffle Hut, but she carried a little bottle of antibacterial gel so she didn't have to go in the bathroom even to wash her hands. It was probably the last place on earth she would ever have sex.

Kiki told Jasmine about the awesome concert and the amazing conversations before and after. She almost didn't mention the phone calls, because she knew Jasmine would blow it all out of proportion, but for some reason she did.

"It's totally some skank-ass ho he keeps on the side," Jasmine fumed. "Or it's a dude! I hear gay guys are always the ones slashing tires."

"Good thing I don't have a car, then," Kiki said, rolling her eyes.

"He could come over here and knife your cat!"

"No one is going to stab Mr. Lister. It's probably just some friend of his looking for . . . oh, I don't know. Maybe they left their wallet in his car or something."

"Don't you want to find out?"

"Well, of course I'd like to know, but if Lyman doesn't tell me—"

"Dude. We're not waiting for anything. Did you get the number?" Jasmine had already whipped out her cell phone.

Kiki flushed, embarrassed to admit that she had memorized the number. It made her seem so stalker.

Jasmine grinned. "You did get it. Good girl."

"It was so easy to remember," Kiki protested. "The first digits are yours, and the last four are Camille's. But what are you going to do? Call and say, 'Hi, I'm Lyman's psycho lady friend's psycho friend, calling to see who the hell you are'?"

"'Course not. Don't you trust me?" Jasmine's eyes were shining.

"Of course not." But Kiki didn't say anything as Jasmine punched the numbers. She felt pretty sure that whoever it was couldn't possibly be awake at this hour—she wouldn't be, if it weren't for Jasmine's early-morning ambush. Even if someone did answer, got suspicious, and called the phone company to see who had made the call, there was no way to connect Jasmine Ash to Kiki Kelvin.

To Kiki's amazement, someone answered on what had to be the second ring.

Jasmine quickly said, "Good morning. Can you confirm that this line is now functional? Is this 594-6260? Yes, we had a complaint that this number was not functioning properly. What is the name on this account? I see. Is it residential or cellular? Well, thank you for choosing us, Mrs. Lyman, and please let us know if you have any problems. Goodbye."

"It was his mother?" Kiki asked when Jasmine clicked off.

"Yep. Mother's cell."

"Wow. How freaky!"

"Freaky?" Jasmine cackled. "You should be glad it's not his gay ex-lover."

"Well, I am glad it's not a gay ex-lover who wants to kill my cat or slash my nonexistent tires, but I'm not happy his mother called thirty times last night either. Weren't you the one saying that home-school boys have weird relationships with their mothers?"

"I say a lot of things, but no one ever takes me seriously."

"That's because you're crazy," Kiki reminded her. "Do you think his mom's crazy?"

"Nah. Probably wanted him to pick up some milk on the way home."

"You're kidding, right?"

"Yes, I am. There is definitely something funny going on there."

"Fantastic," Kiki grumbled.

"Why? What's the problem?"

"The problem is that I really like him."

"*Like* him like him?"

"Yep."

"Oh. That is a problem. When are you going to see him again?"

"Tonight." While they were finishing off their hash browns, Lyman had asked if he could take her to see the Jennifers.

"Aren't you supposed to be at the studio tonight?"

"Yeah, but it's only booked to ten-thirty. Lyman's picking me up there."

"What are you going to do? Go to the opera? Maybe a costume ball at the Belmont Mansion?"

"We're going to hear a band at the End."

"Think he'll wear a tuxedo with a top hat and tails?"

"I have no idea."

"But that's the fun part, isn't it? This Lyman guy is full of surprises."

Kiki was a little worried when 10:55 rolled around and everyone was still hanging around the studio. Mark hadn't said a word to her at the session, not even about her new arrangements. She didn't have anything to say to him, either. Once the session ended, and the three of them plus a couple of sound engineers were sitting on the front steps of the studio, Franklin talked enough for all of them. He chatted with the engineers about mixing the record, and tried to find out from Kiki if Camille was going to Laura Keller's party that night. Franklin rarely noticed guys his own age, but if he saw a guy all dressed up to take Kiki anywhere, she would hear about it forever.

But when Lyman drove up two minutes early, he was wearing jeans and a black hoodie, looking like a perfectly ordinary person. Most guys would not have stenciled the words "Carpe Noctem" on the back of an otherwise plain jacket, but this was normal enough for Kiki. And maybe it was weird for him to get out of the car to open Kiki's door, but not in a bad way.

"Off to go seize the night?" Mark asked Kiki, a little meanly, as she got into the car.

"Off to seize something," she snapped. Lyman shut her door and climbed back into the driver side. Before he could start the engine, she kissed Lyman hello.

"I don't think your bassist likes me," he said, breaking it off. Kiki didn't have to look to know that Mark was glaring at them from the steps.

"I don't care what that boy likes or dislikes."

"So I shouldn't ask any questions about him?"

"Nope." Kiki realized how odd that must sound, so she went on. "We have a lot of history, but as far as I'm concerned, he's just someone I make music with."

"All right. Works for me. Do you need a bite to eat? I think the Jennifers will be onstage pretty soon."

"Nah, I'm fine. And I'd hate to miss the beginning. I love the Jennifers."

"Me, too. Have they signed with a major label yet?"

"I'm not sure. I haven't seen Jennifer C. since we went to Girls Rock Camp, and I haven't seen Jennifer T. since spring sometime. But their demo is awesome. Even my mom likes it."

"She seemed very . . . nice."

"My mom? She's not nice—she's polite. There's a difference. But she's also pretty cool, most of the time. What's your mom like?"

Kiki hadn't planned to bring it up this way, but she couldn't resist such a perfect opportunity.

"My mom? Like you said, polite, but not really nice. Not really cool, either." He shook his head pityingly—it was the same gesture Kiki's physics teacher usually made when she turned in her homework. "She worries a lot. Checks up on me. A lot."

This was Kiki's opening to talk about the freaky phone calls. "Like last night?" she asked innocently.

He sighed. "Like last night."

Kiki put a hand on his knee. "I understand. My parents called me every fifteen minutes when I first went on the road."

"But you were, what, thirteen at the time?"

"Fourteen."

"And your parents got over it, eventually?"

She tilted her head to the side while she thought about it. "Well, yes and no. I think they still worry all the time, but they know I won't answer their phone calls more than twice a day, so they leave it at that. I don't know. I'm an only child, which makes them a little crazy."

"Yeah . . . I know how that can be. But my mom won't stop calling unless she knows exactly where I am at all times."

"So why don't you tell her? Wouldn't that be easier?"

"Maybe." He shrugged and abruptly changed the subject to recording, asking how that night's session went.

"Oh, fine. We're just doing scratch recordings now, so the label has some idea what we want to do on our next album."

She told him all about that, and about the time they recorded in the haunted studio on Music Square East. Kiki never saw any ghosts or anything the two weeks they were there, but there were all sorts of strange echoes and background noise on their thirteenth track.

"Do you believe in ghosts?" he asked her as they pulled into the hidden parking lot behind the End. The only access to the lot was a tiny alley with jagged potholes, and, legal or not, it would be impossible to maneuver a tow truck inside. That Lyman knew about the secret alley impressed Kiki—he really was serious about all kinds of music.

"I think that if ghosts really existed," Kiki said, "scientists would have found some evidence by now. But it took scientists a long time to figure out the whole round Earth thing, too. I guess I have an open mind. What about you?"

"I don't know. But I really like the thought that something about us is still around after death. I'd really hate it if this was it. But if it is . . ."

His voice trailed off as he worked his car into what might be a parking space.

"But if it is?" Kiki prompted him, after he put the car in park. He looked at her, his kaleidoscopic hazel eyes huge and intense.

"But if it is, I mean to make every second count."

For a moment, Kiki thought she and Lyman were going to miss the show, making every second count in the front seat of

ver felt passion like this—from a boy or
greedy for his mouth, his hands, every-
g him set her nerves on fire in a way that
son seem tame and more than a little boring.
ie back door of the club swing open with a
screech, an en somebody plopped down onto the hood of
Lyman's car. Kiki squeaked in surprise, a sound almost completely muffled by Lyman's mouth. They jolted apart and
laughed silently, watching Jennifer T. light up a cigarette and
puff away, completely unaware that the car she was sitting on
was occupied. Kiki knocked on the windshield, scaring Jennifer back to her feet.

"Hey, girly girl," she said, hugging Kiki when she got out
of the car. "What're you doing skulking back here?"

"Just hanging out. Jennifer T., this is my friend Alex
Lyman. Lyman, this is Jennifer T."

"Salutations." He took her fishnet-gloved hand with black-
tipped fingers and kissed it. Jennifer rolled her eyes at Kiki,
but Kiki could see a blush underneath her thick, bone-white
foundation.

"Watch it, kiddo. I don't usually let boys I don't know kiss
me."

"We're almost family, though," Lyman said. "I study with
Jascha Kent."

Jennifer smiled warmly. "Oh! You know Uncle Jascha? How's
he doing? I haven't seen him since he got back from Prague."

"He's all right. I think his new drugs are helping a lot—I
mean, he played Rachmaninoff last night."

"Yeah, Mom told me he was playing the Schermerhorn. We
were in Atlanta for Test Fest. We didn't get home until six

o'clock this morning. I wish I could have been there, though. Was he great?"

"He was great." Kiki and Lyman said it at the same time, like twins. Once again, Kiki found herself holding his hand.

"Well, hey, it's nice to meet you, Lyman. Tell Jascha Jenn says hi. I don't think I'll make it to his place before we hit the road tomorrow. And here, why don't you come in the back way? No reason for you to wait in line. Good seeing you, Kiki. Let's try to have coffee sometime."

"Yeah, let's." Jennifer T. let them into the green room, where Jennifer C. and the other members of the Jennifers (the ones who weren't named Jennifer, whose names Kiki could never remember) were drinking beer and bottled water, listening to the fourth and last opening band.

Kiki led Lyman to the upper level of the club, where there were a few tables, but no dancing, unlike the jammed dance floor below. They sat down at the first free table they saw and he leaned close to her and whispered, "Kiki de Montparnasse."

"What?" She thought she misunderstood him.

"Kiki de Montparnasse. That's who you're named after. The muse who inspired a generation of French painters. The first truly independent woman of the century."

"How on earth did you figure it out?" As far as Kiki knew, her mother was the only person in Nashville who knew who Kiki de Montparnasse was, and she only knew because de Montparnasse was supposed to have been a friend of Josephine Baker, who in turn was supposedly somebody's third cousin once removed. Because Kiki was hard to boss around even as a little kid, her mother had nicknamed her after the notoriously independent Kiki. When she was getting ready to sign her record deal, she hadn't wanted to be mistaken for a certain other young black woman in the industry whose name was Katrina, so Kiki went public with the family nickname.

"What can I say? I've got mad skills," Lyman answered, crossing his arms over his chest like a rap star. "Research skills, but they do come in handy."

"You have got to be the strangest guy I've ever dated."

"Also the hottest?"

"Also the hottest."

"Good." He kissed her, then whispered, "Research isn't the only thing I'm good at."

"Isn't that bad grammar? You can't end a sentence with a preposition."

He stared at her for a second, then burst out laughing. "That sounds like something I would say. It's like we're psychically linked or something."

"Oh, really?" Kiki raised an eyebrow. "What am I thinking right now?" Lyman grinned seductively, but before he could say anything, Kiki said, "No, that's not what I was thinking."

"But you knew exactly what I was thinking. Maybe we *are* soul mates."

She rolled her eyes. "You're a guy. Knitter or not, guys usually are thinking about just one thing."

"But some of us can think about it creatively," he promised. She laughed, and he showed that he really did know what was on her mind: they headed down toward the front of the stage where the Jennifers were already plugging into their amps.

"This first song is dedicated to Miss Kiki Kelvin and her handsome boytoy, Master Alex Lyman," said Jennifer T. from behind her keyboard. "One, two, three, four!"

They launched into a cover of "One Way or Another," and Kiki and Lyman joined the crowd moshing by the stage. It had been a few weeks since Kiki had been on the other side of a stage during a show, and she was loving it. As much as she loved drumming, it was still a performance, something she did for the crowd as well as for herself. But dancing with Lyman was pure pleasure.

After a thirty-minute set and two encores, Lyman and Kiki snuck out the back, declining an offer to go clubbing with Jennifer C. and her drummer in favor of coffee and doughnuts at Krispy Kreme.

"Better let Mom know where we're headed first," Lyman told her, typing out a quick text message as they walked down Elliston Place.

"Does that mean she won't be calling?"

"Hopefully."

When they got to Krispy Kreme, they had to watch the doughnut conveyer for ten minutes while they waited for a table. The restaurant was crammed with urban cowboys and dixie chicks fresh from the honky-tonks on Second Avenue, goths who had just left the Maze, hip-hop fans, ravers, and everyone else who needed a snack at 1:00 AM. Kiki and Lyman killed time by having thumb wars.

After they finally got a table and a cup of coffee and two plain, glazed doughnuts each, still hot enough to burn Kiki's mouth, Kiki saw Lyman's face turn absolutely gray as he stared at something or someone behind her.

"Is it Mark?" she asked, turning to face the door. But it wasn't Mark. It was a small, thin, middle-aged woman with mad, curly brown hair. Kiki had never seen her before, but Kiki had a pretty good idea who she was.

"Alex!" the woman called, marching over to their table.

"Hi, Mom." He slid over, and his mother wedged herself into the booth next to him. "Kiki, this is my mom. Mom, this is Kiki Kelvin."

"Nice to meet you," Kiki lied.

"Likewise," said Mrs. Lyman. Her eyes were a poisonous green, like a squashed caterpillar. Otherwise, she looked a lot like her son.

"So . . . come here often?" Kiki asked, trying to sound innocent while she kicked Lyman savagely in the ankle.

"All the time," said Mrs. Lyman, looking around. She was so thin the bones of her wrist looked like they pressed through the skin—and no one that thin spent a lot of time at Krispy Kreme.

"So you just happened to be in the neighborhood?" Kiki asked, wondering why Lyman's mother would have driven all the way to Krispy Kreme in the middle of the night. Her parents were paranoid, but even they had never shown up while she was on a date.

"Exactly."

"Okay." Kiki bit her tongue so that she didn't add, "If you say so." Kiki wasn't much of a liar, but she was a lot better than Mrs. Lyman. Still, she smiled at the older woman as sweetly as she could. She had never met a mother she couldn't charm. Not once.

"So, tell me, Kiki, are your parents employed?"

Kiki had to grit her teeth to keep her jaw from dropping. What kind of question was that? A racist question, whispered a voice in the back of Kiki's mind. She couldn't help thinking that if she were white, Mrs. Lyman would have asked, "What

do your parents do?" instead of "Do your parents do anything?"

"Dad's a doctor of neurology and Mom's a judge," she said
quietly, watching carefully for Mrs. Lyman's reaction. She didn't
look surprised, which was a relief. But her questions continued.

"Family court?"

"Juvenile."

"Which district?"

"Why?"

"Excuse me?"

"I said, 'Why?' What difference does it make which district
Mom represents?"

Mrs. Lyman sniffed huffily. "I was just making conversation."

Kiki took a deep breath and let it out slowly. Then she
cranked up the wattage on her smile and said, "What about
you? What do you do?"

"I'm a mother." She said it as if it was the only possible job
a woman should have.

While Kiki quietly seethed, Mrs. Lyman went on, "I also
help manage Alex's musical career. He's very talented, you know.
I understand that you're also interested in music?"

"I'm working on my second album with RGB Records."
Kiki almost mentioned the sales figures on their first album,
the fact that they were on the cover of *Billboard*, and the
rumors at RGB that Temporary Insanity would be on *David
Letterman* two months after the new record came out—but she
didn't get a chance.

"Oh, yes. I hear you were on the road for three months with

two boys. Did you have a hotel room, or did you all sleep together on the bus?"

Kiki couldn't take it a moment longer. She faced Lyman directly. "Can I talk to you a second?"

"Sure."

Rather than try to budge his mother, he ducked under the table and followed Kiki outside.

"What is your mother doing here?" Kiki demanded.

"What do you think she's doing?"

"I think she's trying to decide whether I'm worthy to date her son, which is maybe just a little premature, since this is our second date."

"My mom worries a lot. I told you that before."

"You didn't say she'd be joining us, though."

"I didn't know! I didn't think she'd actually show up!"

"Well, are you going to tell her to get lost?"

He looked shocked, and more than a little sick. "I can't tell her that."

"Yes, you can. It's very easy. 'Mom, I love you, but go away.' Simple."

"I could say it, I guess, but I can't make her do anything." He shook his head sadly and added, "She's more than a little nuts."

"Either your mother goes home, or I do. Right now."

"Whatever you say." He stomped back into the restaurant where his mother was still sitting quietly with their cooling coffee and doughnuts. He came back with his jacket and keys.

Kiki stared at him, stunned that he chose ending his date with her over saying something to his mother. She climbed into his car without a word, and didn't say anything on the long drive back to her house. Every now and then Lyman would say, "What you've got to understand is . . ." or, "The thing about Mom is . . ." but he couldn't quite finish a sentence.

He pulled up half a block from her driveway, obviously hoping they could have another make-out session out of sight of her house. That's when Kiki found her voice, though it was shaking with anger.

"My house is up there, Lyman."

He just sighed again and drove up to her driveway.

"Kiki, I'm sorry, but there's a lot you don't understand about me and my mom," he said miserably, unable to meet her eyes.

"Yeah, I hear home-school boys have really close relationships with their mothers. So why don't you go hook up with her?"

Lyman looked shocked, and then winced. He started to answer her, but she slammed out of his car before she could hear one whiny word.

"Have a nice time?" her mother called as she stalked past the master bedroom.

"Spectacular!" Kiki answered. She didn't know if her mother realized she was being sarcastic or not—her mom was probably half-asleep anyway, too tired to care.

"Psychically linked," Kiki muttered a few minutes later, kicking off her shoes. One of them scuffed the paint on her door, which she'd hear about later, but just then she didn't care. How could a date go from so good to so bad so fast? No guy was worth dealing with a mother like that, not even Mark—and besides, Mark's mother loved Kiki a lot more than Mark did.

Boy Shopping

She flopped onto the bed and turned on her cell phone so she could tell Jasmine that she was right about home-school boys, but a text message popped up before she could dial Jasmine's number.

I can explain. Pls come back outside?

Kiki chewed on her lower lip, still slightly raw from kissing, and tried to decide if Lyman was worth a second chance. She felt like she had found the perfect pair of jeans, perfect color, perfect cut, perfectly worn in, but the price was more than she wanted to pay. What was she going to do?

SHOULD KIKI TRY HIM ON?
Turn to page 107 to see if Lyman's her perfect fit.

SHOULD KIKI PUT HIM BACK ON THE RACK?
Turn to page 115 to see what happens if she tells him goodbye.

What happens when Kiki gives Lyman a second chance?
Read on to find out!

✳ Chapter 6 ✳

Seizing the Night

"Thanks for giving me a chance to explain," Lyman said, sliding off the trunk of his car. Even in the orange light of the streetlamps Lyman looked great. Kiki had to remind herself that no matter how cute he was, his mother was still out there somewhere. For all she knew, Mrs. Lyman might be speeding toward her house that very minute.

"Okay, talk," Kiki said, folding her arms over her chest. Her bare feet were firmly planted on the driveway with plenty of space between her and Lyman. She wasn't going to let him charm her into forgetting about how awful the evening turned out. She didn't really believe any explanation would excuse Mrs. Lyman's meanness and his complete unwillingness to do anything about it, but Kiki thought it was only fair to give him a chance.

"Ah, okay. Um." Lyman was staring at his feet as if his black sneakers were doing something interesting.

"Lyman, it's late, and I know you know a whole lot of words. So talk already."

"All right. Well . . . His voice petered out like a snuffed candle.

Kiki was about to give up and go back inside when he said, very quietly, "My brothers died in a car accident last year."

"What?" Kiki asked, sure she had misheard.

"My older brothers, Scott and Nicky, were in a car accident last year. In May. The fifth of May, to be exact, at eight twenty-two AM."

"Oh, my God! I'm so sorry!" Thinking back, Kiki could remember hearing about it on the news. It was a terrible accident involving a tractor-trailer and two brothers on the way to school.

"Yeah . . ." His voice trailed off again, and they were both silent for a minute. Then Kiki walked up to him and gave him a hug.

"Mom was pretty weird before it happened," he said, resting his head on her shoulder. "But since then she's been a lot worse."

"I understand," she said, though she knew that wasn't really true.

"I'm not saying that I think what Mom does is okay," he continued. "And I don't think she's going to change any time soon. But I wanted you to know that it doesn't have anything to do with you really, and now that she's met you, at least, she'll probably settle down a little."

"Do you really think so?"

He shrugged and said in a small voice, "Maybe."

"Okay, I guess," Kiki said slowly. Of course, it wasn't really okay with her that she and Lyman could be stalked by his mother, but what else could she say? "I guess we'll work it out somehow."

Knowing that her parents might well be watching from their darkened bedroom upstairs, Kiki gave him a quick kiss good-bye and told him she would call him tomorrow.

"I'm looking forward to it," he said, climbing back into his car. Kiki waved and let herself back into the house. Her parents were silent when she passed their door this time, which was just as well, since she was not in the mood for talking. Knowing the truth—and how much Lyman liked her—made it much easier for her to fall asleep, even with all the complications.

By the next morning, however, Kiki did want to talk about the situation, but not with her parents or the Pussycat Posse. Her parents would make too much of the potential danger of Mrs. Lyman's obsessive behavior, and the Pussycats would not make enough of it. None of them had ever been stalked, so they could never know what it meant to willingly invite a stalker to become a part of one's life. One of her friends knew exactly what that meant. Unfortunately, he was barely speaking to her.

"Are we still best friends or what?" Kiki asked when Mark answered her call. She was still in her pajamas and had yet to actually get out of bed, and she figured he was in the same state. Even if there was still tension between them, she hoped he would be too sleepy to fight.

"Still best friends," Mark said, yawning.

"Cool. I need to talk to you."

"Now?" Mark still sounded tired, but not shocked. This wasn't the first Sunday morning that began with his cell phone ringing.

"Soon."

"I'll come and get you as soon as I'm dressed," he promised.

"Great."

By the time his Karmann Ghia rattled into her driveway, Kiki was dressed and waiting.

"We need to talk," he said as she let herself into his car.

"Um, yeah," she admitted. "Here's what I've been thinking—"

"I love you."

"*What?*" It was a good thing he was driving, not Kiki, because she would have driven straight into a tree. At any point in the last three years, those words would have made Kiki's heart explode with happiness. But now that she had found someone else, Mark had finally decided that she was the one. She didn't know what to think about his revelation. She knew how she felt, though: confused.

"I love you," he repeated, calmly avoiding all the trees lining Kiki's street. "I've always loved you, I guess. I had never really thought about it until the other morning, when you said what you did about being stalked. It freaked me out completely to think that you could be in danger."

"Why didn't you say something then?" Her confusion was shading to anger. But then she realized that if he had spoken up, she never would have met Lyman, never would have learned the difference between love and passion. But now she did know the difference. It was too late.

"I almost did, that night, after the fight," Mark admitted. "But everything had just gotten back to normal, and I didn't want to risk our friendship, the band, everything we have, if you didn't feel the same way."

"Mark! Did you really think I would say, 'Nope, not interested, don't ever speak to me again?' You didn't think we'd find a way to work through it?" As soon as she said it, though, Kiki realized that she had feared exactly the same reaction from him. Otherwise, she would have said something herself. She wasn't being fair to him, but she didn't think it was fair of him to spring this on her now.

"I didn't know what you were going to say. I tried to get Jasmine to tell me what you were thinking, but she weaseled out of every question. But I guess it's pretty obvious how you feel, huh?" Mark's voice almost creaked with bitterness.

"Hey," Kiki said gently, squeezing his elbow. "You're my best friend. But I'm not in love with you, not really. I thought I was, until recently, but I was wrong."

"Because of this Lyman guy?"

"Lyman and I have our own problems. That's why I called you in the first place. But as much as I love you, Mark, I'm not in love. That's all there is to it."

"So what's the story with him?"

Kiki hesitated—if she were in Mark's position, the last thing she would want to hear was her complaining about her romantic problems. But if they were going to be friends for real, just friends, for ever and ever, she had to trust him with just this sort of problem. So she told him about Lyman and his mother as Mark drove around and around Kiki's neighborhood.

"Think *she'll* send you a cow heart on Valentine's Day?" he asked when she got to the end of the story.

Kiki shuddered. "I hope not." She slapped the dashboard in frustration. "I hate this. I feel this incredible connection with him, but I don't think I can deal with that woman showing up when we're having a bite to eat or catching a show. I feel sorry for her, of course, but she was pretty nasty."

"I hate to say it, but honestly, Kiki, if you really care for this guy you'll find a way to deal with it. Unless you think you're actually in real danger, like she might come after you with a knife, then I think maybe you have to try to handle it."

"I know you're right, but how am I supposed to deal with it?"

He shrugged, his eyes glued to the road, the way they had been throughout the conversation. "You're smart. You'll think of something."

When Mark dropped her off at home a little while later, she kissed him lightly on the cheek.

"You know, if you change your mind," he said, "I'll still be here. And I'll always be your friend."

"Thanks, Mark. I know."

Kiki went back inside and gave Lyman a call.

"So where are you going tonight?" Sasha asked a month later, watching Kiki tie on a pair of hiking boots.

"The ballet?" Jasmine suggested. By now the Pussycat Posse knew Lyman's eclectic tastes.

"It's a surprise."

"What do you do to get all these surprises?" Jasmine stared jealously at the stack of CDs and DVDs collecting on Kiki's desk.

"Wouldn't you like to know."

"Actually, I would."

"Well, the secret is—" Kiki paused for effect.

"WHAT?" Jasmine, Camille and Sasha all leaned in to hear.

"The secret is that Lyman and I do pretty much what everyone else does. But we do it creatively."

"What's that supposed to mean?" Jasmine groaned.

"It means that there are benefits to dating someone with research skills."

"Huh?" Camille asked.

"Never mind." Kiki grinned smugly.

"So is Mama joining you?" Camille asked.

"Nope!" Kiki declared happily. Over the last month, Lyman's mother had gotten more used to the idea of Lyman dating. She still called him all the time, but she never showed up on their dates. Kiki figured Lyman had laid down the law about that. As long as Lyman called as soon as he arrived at her house, as soon as they got to their destination, and to let his mom know he was heading for home, she didn't stalk them. Much.

It was a start anyway.

"I've got a surprise for you," Lyman said after kissing her hello.

"How surprising," Kiki purred.

"It's on the back seat."

Instead of the thin box containing yet another movie that Lyman thought she had to see, there was a small, round bundle wrapped in silver paper about the size of her fist.

"What is it?" she asked, snagging the ribbon on her index finger.

"Open it up."

"But anticipation is such a turn-on." She shook it to see if it rattled. It didn't. It wasn't quite the right shape for a jewelry box, and it was too soft. She couldn't imagine what it was.

"If that's how you feel, it can wait." He reached to take the present back.

Boy Shopping

"Are you kidding?"

She ripped it open, and two long, soft fingerless gloves fell into her lap. They were black and silver striped, and soft as snow on her arms, which they covered almost to her shoulders.

"They're gorgeous!"

"Thank you." He added, in a fake-pompous voice, "Didn't I tell you that there were advantages to dating a knitter?"

"I'm sure you did." She brushed the side of his face with her gloved palm. "These are really nice. They're so soft." She stroked the back of his neck. "So silky."

"I hate to say this, but if you don't want me to pull over right now, you need to stop."

"Maybe I *want* you to pull over right now." But after tracing the back of his ear with the back of her hand, she folded her hands in her lap. She was too curious about their secret destination to distract him completely.

"So where are we going?" she asked, once Lyman was breathing normally again.

"Radnor Lake. If Mom thinks she can find us in the woods, she's welcome to try, but I think it'll be pretty private."

"Sounds perfect," she said, settling into her seat.

"Everything sounds perfect when you're around. We make beautiful music together, Kiki Kelvin."

"It's true." She grinned. "We're a perfect fit."

Kiki seems pretty happy, but what if Lyman isn't the only boy for her? Turn to page 115 to see what happens if she decides to dump him, or back to page 57 to choose another boy for her.

You think that Kiki would be better off without Lyman?
Read on to find out what happens when she says goodbye.

✳ Chapter 6 ✳

Very Necessary

"Look, Lyman," she said as gently as she could, though she was more than a little annoyed. At least on a cell phone he couldn't see the face she was making. "You're a cool guy, and I liked hanging with you, but your mom is crazy."

"I know that. But if I could tell you why—"

"It doesn't really matter why your mom is such a nut, unless you think she's going to change. Is she?"

"Probably not any time soon."

"And are you going to tell her to back off?" Kiki asked. She waited for Lyman to respond. When he didn't she said, "Okay. I'm sorry for you, but I just can't deal with that kind of crap. I've got enough psychos in my life. Goodbye."

"Goodbye."

Kiki sighed, glad she didn't have to do the whole can-we-still-be-friends thing. Clearly, she was doomed to be alone.

"Learn to like being single," she told her reflection as she washed up. Without makeup, she noticed how tired she looked—

her dark circles were beginning to look like bruises. "Being alone is good. Really. A little alone time is exactly what you need."

She turned off her cell phone and went straight to bed.

The next day she left her phone off. She would tell the Pussycats the whole horror story on Monday. Meanwhile she was going to learn to enjoy being alone. She locked herself in her bedroom and did piles of homework, had pizza with her parents, and finally changed out of her pajamas and into jeans.

"Where are you headed?" her father asked when he saw her snagging the keys to her bike lock from the kitchen junk drawer.

"The Wentworth playground."

"Should I even ask why?"

"I'm going to write," she said, showing him the spiral-bound notebooks in her backpack.

"You have school in the morning. You need to be home by ten-thirty."

"Fine, Dad. Whatever."

She pedaled through the darkness, ignoring the harsh bite of autumn wind whipping through her dreadlocks.

Once she got to the lower school's playground, she ignored the swings and monkey bars, heading straight for the tree house. When she was small, she never got to play up there. The popular kids, which included Camille and Sasha even then, were always hogging it. She and Mark would be in a corner somewhere, making up some complicated game of "let's pretend," where they were magical scientist rock stars, or something.

As if thinking about him was enough to make him appear,

Kiki heard his car wheezing before it rolled into sight, pulling into the parking lot before it collapsed into silence.

She clicked off her flashlight and watched Mark get out of the car, grabbing his elderly gray backpack before gently shutting the door.

"Hey," she called, spooking him badly as he climbed the tree house ladder.

"What are you doing here?" he asked when he'd climbed in and joined Kiki, who was leaning against a tree branch.

"Same thing you're doing, probably. Writing."

"Yeah." He took a notebook out of his bag, but he didn't write a word. Neither did Kiki. They just stared at each other in the dark.

"So, about the other night—"

"It's okay, Mark. You can go out with Jasmine if you want." Knowing that Jasmine wasn't interested made it easier for Kiki to say, but it was more or less true.

"That's not what I was going to say."

"I know."

"Then what was I going to say?" He couldn't have sounded more sarcastic, but Kiki was used to that from him. He always got sarcastic or mean when he felt cornered. He had said some of his funniest lines ever when other kids were teasing him, even back in kindergarten. It spooked Kiki sometimes to realize how long she had known him.

"You were going to say that you were sorry if you were rude last night about Lyman," Kiki told him. "But you aren't really sorry—you were just freaked out, especially since I saw you with Jasmine when I was out with him, and seeing the two of you obviously freaked me out. But since Lyman and I aren't going to keep seeing each other, that part doesn't really matter, and I wanted to let you know that you are free to date Jasmine if you want. Not that I could stop you anyway."

"Okay, maybe you did know what I was going to say."

"Get a clue, Mark—I always know what you're going to say. Well, almost always."

He shrugged. "We've known each other practically forever."

"Yeah. Maybe we're psychically linked." Kiki knew she sounded more than a little bitter.

"I don't know. I have a hard time reading you sometimes."

"I'm not a book, Mark!" Kiki yelled, as all of her mixed-up feelings about Mark flooded through her. "You don't have to read me. If you want to know what I'm thinking, ask! I'm right here!"

Kiki could see his cheeks turning red, even in the moonlight.

"Fine! What are you thinking, Kiki? Why are you screaming at me?"

"You really want to know?" She didn't wait for an answer. She just kissed him. It was nothing like kissing Lyman for the first time. This wasn't a soft, slow exploration. She bruised her lips against his, nipped his tongue hard enough to make him cry out. For a second he just sat there, then she felt an arm tightening around her waist while his other hand plunged into her hair, holding her closer to him.

"I guess I should ask what's on your mind a little more often, huh?" he asked a few minutes later as they angled for a more comfortable position.

"It's better than asking out Jasmine to see if you can get her to tell you how I feel."

"She figured it out, huh? I thought I was being subtle."

"No, she thinks you're gay. I figured it out, 'cause I know you that well." She didn't mention that she had figured it out about ten seconds before she said it, though it seemed obvious now. Even if Mark were interested in Jasmine, she wouldn't waste a lot of energy being nice to him. And Mark was more than a little shy about asking girls out—otherwise he and Kiki would have gotten together a long time before.

"Oh yeah? What am I thinking?"

She kissed him again and started to unbutton his shirt. His eyes widened when he realized her intention. He hesitated for only a moment, then his hands caressed and explored her. *We're really doing this!* screamed in Kiki's brain, until she couldn't think at all.

Being with Mark was like discovering a whole new country hidden in her bedroom closet: perfectly familiar, perfectly safe, yet completely new and exciting. Kiki really did feel close to Mark in a whole new way, really felt she understood him on a whole new level. She thought she might cry when it was over, but instead she found herself laughing, her head pillowed on his chest. To her surprise, he joined in, both of them giggling like a pair of kindergartners.

"What are you laughing at?" Kiki asked when she had caught her breath.

"Oh, nothing."

"Really?"

He planted a kiss on the top of her head. "Nothing, really.

I just thought it was funny that you really did know exactly what I was thinking."

Kiki doesn't regret dumping Lyman—do you? Turn to page 107 to see what would happen if she decided to stay with him, or to page 57 to choose another boy.

* Chapter 4 *
Jacob

Kiki stayed up late working on her e-mail, distracted while she typed by the picture on his HelloHello profile. Jacob Young! What kind of mind lay behind his honey-brown eyes, which Kiki remembered from the days before he started wearing sunglasses. And that face! It could have been carved from the same mahogany as her father's most prized African mask, polished to the same satiny smoothness. In the morning her mother had to shake her twice before she crawled out of bed and over to her computer. There was an e-mail from Jacob, just two lines long: "What are you doing Friday night? Let's hit the Trip-Hop Triple Threat."

Friday was the one night Kiki was almost always off—the band didn't play on Fridays unless they had a show, and since their contract allowed them to travel only one weekend a month during the school year, they played big gigs in town and, very occasionally, opened for a bigger act at the Ryman or Starwood.

It annoyed Kiki to admit that she didn't have plans, but it was the only night she did have free for the next couple of weeks, so she e-mailed Jacob to say he could pick her up at 7:30. She was a little hurt that he hadn't spent more time on his message to her, but those two lines were the most anyone had gotten out of Jacob Young since they started ninth grade, so she decided she ought to be thankful.

An hour later, Kiki passed Jacob in the hallway as she hurried to English class. She smiled, waved, and almost said something, but his face was just as expressionless behind his sunglasses as it always was. Kiki thought he actually sped up a little after they passed one another, as if he was afraid she would run after him.

"Did I just get dissed?" she asked Sasha, who was jogging along with her. Their English classroom was a long way from homeroom.

Sasha's long violet curls and her lacy black skirt streamed behind her. Sometimes Kiki wondered if that was the difference between goth and punk: she and Sasha both dressed in black most of the time, but Kiki rarely wore anything covered in lace.

"I don't think so. I mean, why would he do that after he asked you out?" Sasha asked, waving hello to Dr. Bonner, their AP European History teacher, as they passed the history wing.

"I don't know, but that felt like a diss."

"Maybe he didn't see you?" Sasha sounded doubtful.

"Maybe he's secretly blind. At least that would explain the sunglasses."

"Maybe he's mute? Then he'd have to meet girls online."

Kiki laughed, the bell rang, and they ran the rest of the way to English class.

Kiki was actually beginning to wonder if someone had used Jacob's name and picture to pick up girls on the Internet, when the secretary paged Kiki to the office during fifth period European History class.

"What have you done now, Kelvin?" Dr. Bonner asked. Everyone was staring at her, except for Mark. He refused to look up from the chapter on Charlemagne they were supposed to be reading. They might not be fighting anymore, but they weren't on the friendliest terms either, not since he'd asked about Jasmine.

"I haven't done anything!" she insisted. She was expecting the worst, though, when she got to the office. Could it have anything to do with the hijacked PA system Monday morning?

"Kiki, this has to be signed for." The secretary handed her a long florist's box, the kind that she'd only seen in movies, filled with roses.

Kiki balanced the box of flowers in one arm as she scrawled her name on the form the delivery guy handed her. Then she opened the box. The roses were a strange bronzy-brownish-pink, almost the exact color of the skin on the inside of her wrist. Kiki had received plenty of roses in the last few years, from her fans and from RGB, but they were always white, pink, or red. She had never seen roses this color before.

"Ooooh, chocolate roses," cooed the secretary.

"I can't find a card," Kiki said.

"I guess you have a secret admirer," the secretary said.

"I guess so," Kiki admitted. "Would you mind putting them in the fridge until two-thirty?"

"Just don't forget them."

"I won't forget." When Kiki stepped out of the office, Jacob Young was strolling down the hall. He turned to her, gave her a slow nod, and kept going. He was the one who had sent the roses—Kiki was certain. She felt a flush creeping across her whole body. Jacob Young really *was* into her. It was like hearing that instead of getting you a new ten-speed for your birthday, your parents decided to get you a Porsche: that unbelievable.

The Pussycats all purred happily when they saw Kiki's roses at the end of the day, except for Jasmine.

"They might not even be from Jacob," Jasmine said as they all walked to the parking lot.

"You think those are from Jacob?" Mark asked, popping up behind them.

"Did *you* send them, Mark?" Jasmine asked, turning on him as fast as a rattlesnake. "Is this your way of declaring your everlasting love for Kiki?"

"I, um, no," he said, turning purple.

"That's enough, Jazz. Come on, Mark. Let's get going."

Kiki dragged him by the elbow to his car as the Pussycat Posse laughed behind them. Jasmine laughed loudest of all.

"So, I, um, Kiki," he began, but she cut him off.

"Mark, forget what Jasmine said. She just likes messing with you."

"Um, yeah. So, um, are those really from Jacob?"

"Yes."

"Oh. That's . . . cool, I guess."

Kiki almost said, "You had your chance," but why should she bother? If he had suddenly decided that she was the one, it was too late. She was going out with Jacob that Friday night no matter what. If Mark finally got it together to ask her out, he'd have his chance, too. Later. If Jacob wasn't her soul mate.

By the time Friday night rolled around, Kiki was having second thoughts about Jacob. Well, more like tenth or eleventh thoughts, since he kept ignoring her in the halls all week. What was his problem? He couldn't possibly be embarrassed to be seen with her—could he? He was Jacob Young, who may or may not have been in *Hustle and Flow*, and was definitely the son of producer Andre "Too" Young, but she was Kiki Kelvin— she had been on the cover of *Billboard* twice before her seventeenth birthday! And if he really was embarrassed to be seen with her, then why were they going to Trip-Hop Triple Threat at the Maze, where half of Wentworth would probably turn up? Kiki had no idea what was going on, and she wasn't about to ask him. Instead, she just laced up her lucky Doc Martens, tucked them under a nice new pair of low-rise jeans, checked her tank top to make sure her bra straps were covered, and went downstairs to wait for Jacob to show up.

"Since when have you liked Jacob Young?" her dad asked, wandering through the living room on his way to the garage. For once, he and Kiki's mom weren't going to see her off on a date. Since they had known Jacob's parents since Kiki was in kindergarten, they didn't think he was much of a threat. This had less to do with any faith in Jacob himself than the fact that if Dr. Kelvin wanted to hunt Jacob down, he knew exactly where he lived.

"I've always liked Jacob."

"No, you used to think he was nasty."

"That's because he ate glue."

"Just for fun?"

"I think it was a dare."

"Booger-eater?"

"Maybe. I can't remember." It was hard enough believing that Jacob had anything to do with the faintly disgusting first grader he had been, much less remembering exactly what he had done. Kiki thought all boys were gross back then, except for Mark, and he'd had his moments too.

"Right. Well, think about that before you let him stick his tongue in your mouth."

Kiki groaned. "Have a nice night, Dad."

"You too. I'll see you at two o'clock, or I'll come looking."

"Goodnight, Dad!"

"Okay, goodnight."

Jacob showed up ten minutes later, looking like he did every day at school, but better. The sunglasses were gone, revealing a pair of eyes the color of old gold, eyes that were a lot more mesmerizing than they had been in elementary school.

"Hey," Kiki said, climbing into the passenger seat of a new Z3 convertible, perfectly black inside and out. He drove a black Mercedes sedan to school, which was nice enough, but this car was a work of art, especially the sound system. Gnarls Barkley was pouring through the speakers like molasses, dark and sweet.

"Hey." It was the first word he had spoken to her since they were twelve. And it was the last she heard for a while, since he reversed out of Kiki's driveway fast enough to knock the breath from her lungs, then whipped through the curvy streets of Belle Meade, her quiet, tree-lined neighborhood, so fast that wind was all Kiki could hear. A quick glance at their reflection in the window of a car they passed told Kiki that they looked like a scene from a movie: the rapper who has just made it to the top, but can't forget his past; the gold digger who may leave him for the next big star, but will always love him. It would be a movie with great beats and a sad ending—him dead, her pregnant, something like that. Kiki had to laugh, but that sound too was lost in the wind roiling around Jacob's car.

"What's so funny?" he asked when they stopped at a light.

"Just thinking about how different things look from outside."

"I know what you mean." He nodded at the car stopped next to theirs, an elderly Cadillac full of elderly white people. "They probably think I'm a drug dealer and you're some kind of ho."

"We're not wearing enough jewelry." Jacob wasn't wearing any, and Kiki just had on a pair of tiny diamond studs.

"Look at them. That's what they see."

Kiki saw that he was probably right. The old man driving the car was staring at them as if staring might make their heads explode, and the three women in the car wouldn't even look at them. Maybe the old man had some reason for giving them the look of death, but if he wasn't an out-and-out racist, convinced that any young black couple driving around Belle Meade in a new BMW had to be drug dealers, Kiki didn't know what his problem was.

The light changed, and the chance for conversation was left back at the intersection with the old, slow Cadillac. When they got to the little Mexican place next to the Maze, they had plenty of time to talk, but Jacob had retreated into his shell of silence.

At first Kiki tried asking him questions, easy, open-ended questions, like reporters always ask at the beginning of an interview, but he would answer with as few words as possible, and that was that. If he was completely silent around a girl he had known his entire life, Kiki understood why he had tried HelloHello.

Kiki stared at her burrito as if she could see Mother Teresa's face burned into the tortilla, feeling her stomach jump around. When she was with Mark and Franklin, silence always meant something was wrong—most of the time the two of them talked nonstop.

"Can I ask you a weird question?" Kiki asked. She knew, even before she asked, that she was being stupid. Guys don't like having relationship talks when they are actually in a relationship, much less when they're on a first date. But it wasn't like Jacob could shut her out anymore than he was already, so what difference did it make? And it was something she'd been thinking about a lot lately—might as well get a guy's opinion.

"Do you think people can be destined for each other? A *Romeo and Juliet* sort of deal?"

Kiki expected him to say no, or sit there in silence. Instead he put down his fork, pinned her with his golden eyes, and said, "Romeo and Juliet are the dumbest characters in that whole play. The only character with anything going on at all is Mercutio, and he dies for it."

Kiki cocked her head, considering his answer. "Yeah, I guess that's true," she admitted. She probably should have used a different example, or have phrased the question better. "But what about true love? Not love at first sight, or whatever, but the whole twin souls thing?"

"Absolutely." His eyes glowed like lamps. Kiki knew she was blushing. She couldn't help it. Whenever he looked at her—really looked at her—she felt as if she was bathed in a golden spotlight all her own.

"How do you—would you—know?" she asked. "How could you tell if it was the real thing?"

He ate another couple of bites of his tostada, and Kiki thought at first that he was giving her the silent treatment again, but realized he was giving her question serious consideration.

After a few minutes, he gave her the The Look again. "You remember reading *Catcher in the Rye* back in eighth grade?"

"Sure." Jacob may not talk in class, but he had obviously been paying attention.

"Holden says that the thing about him and Jane is that he doesn't have to talk when she's around. They can just sit there and understand."

"I guess I had forgotten that part."

He nodded. "Most people are just talk. Not everything is about words."

Kiki nodded too, but she wasn't sure she really understood. After all, Jacob didn't really talk to anybody—how would he know whether someone understood him?

At that point their waiter came by with the bill. He wasn't much older than they were. "I was just waiting for a break in the conversation," the waiter joked, winking at Kiki. La Rosa was small and cozy, and the tables were barely large enough for two placemats—perfect for a night of low-key romance. Every other table in the restaurant buzzed with romantic whispers or loud laughter. There had probably never been a date as silent as this one, at least not at La Rosa.

"Man, you guys just can't shut up," the waiter teased. "I can tell you guys have been going out forever."

Jacob gave him a look that made him take a step back and begin stammering an apology.

"Forget it, man." Jacob handed him a credit card without even glancing at the bill. The waiter scurried to the back of the restaurant so fast the other diners probably thought Jacob had threatened him.

It took all of three minutes to walk from La Rosa to the Maze, though Kiki wouldn't have wanted to walk it by herself—it was on a sketchy corner near the edge of downtown. She had no fears walking with Jacob, though. It amazed her how he could say more with a look than someone like Mark could say with a hundred three-syllable words.

Inside the club, Triple Threat had already begun. The cinder-block walls were thumping with complex beats overlaid by honey-sweet vocals and samples from what sounded like a string quartet.

"The acoustics here are better than you would think," Kiki said.

"It's not the building. It's the speakers. They've got Khartoum speakers, this German company that makes movie theater sound equipment, and triplex placement." Jacob went on, but that was the only part Kiki understood. And she wasn't dumb about sound systems—after more than three hundred sound checks, you learn a thing or two about music amplification. But Jacob was an expert. He may not have normal conversations but he could definitely lecture her about various amps. Not that she minded—it was a subject that interested her almost as much as it fascinated him.

Kiki was about to ask him if he knew what kind of equipment was necessary to pull the morning announcements prank at school, when they got to the head of the line and flashed their fakes. Kiki almost never used a fake ID, since most bouncers in Nashville knew exactly how old she was and were willing to let her in anyway, but she didn't make it to the Maze often.

"You want a drink?" Jacob asked.

"Not really." The Maze had beer, but no hard liquor. Kiki would drink a beer if it was cold enough and she was thirsty enough, but she would rather have Jack and Coke, or even a glass of water.

"That's cool." Jacob bought two bottles of water, handed one to Kiki, then headed further into the dark, twisty halls that gave the club its name. To keep up with each other they had to hold hands, and from there the next step was dancing. Kiki had never danced with anyone who moved like Jacob. It figured, since his mother had danced in videos back in the '80s—that's how she met his father. But there was a world of difference between what Mrs. Young did in the background of Madonna videos and how Jacob moved across the Maze's main dance floor. It wasn't anything flashy or crazy—he didn't crowd the other dancers, or make Kiki look like she was dancing by herself. He just always knew the right way to move: when to step right, when to pause, when to press Kiki so close she could feel his heart slamming against his ribs, when to give her a little space.

Soon all of the little worries that had been knocking around Kiki's brain—was Jacob too shy, too quiet, too weird?—were lost in the beat that moved Kiki, Jacob, and everyone else in the club. They danced through the end of the first set, danced to the recorded tracks that were played while the second group set up, and through the entire second set. They definitely didn't need words for this kind of communication.

Sweat glued dreads to the back of Kiki's neck, and even after she finished off her bottle of water, she felt like she was overheating. Grinding against Jacob for the full six minutes of "Demonology" would have overheated Kiki in a walk-in freezer, much less in a hot, smoky club.

"I think I need some air," Kiki said. She had to repeat herself twice, she was so breathless.

After making sure they hadn't sweated their hand stamps clean off, they threaded their way back out of the Maze and into the parking lot.

"'Demonology' is such a great song," Kiki said, fanning herself with her empty water bottle.

"It's their best, except maybe for 'Talking Pictures,' on *Fictional*. That whole album drops it."

"You like it better than *Triggerfinger?*"

"Too different to compare."

Jacob had as much to say about music itself as he did about sound systems, and not just hip-hop and trip-hop. He knew plenty about the local rock scene, and knew the Temporary Insanity playlists almost as well as Kiki did. She couldn't stop smiling, even though Jacob hadn't lost the closed-off look he'd worn all day. They really did have a lot in common. They really did understand each other. And if dancing with Jacob in a room full of people was enough to make Kiki light-headed, she couldn't imagine what it would be like to be with him behind closed doors.

Jacob

Kiki was trying to maneuver the conversation from the show to where they might find a little privacy afterwards, when she heard giggles coming from somewhere nearby, probably behind a car, followed by three very familiar voices, raised in chorus.

"Kiki and Jacob, sitting in a tree, K-I-S-S-I-N-G. First comes love, then comes marriage, then comes Kiki with a baby carriage!"

"All right, get out here," Kiki growled. "Jazz, Sasha, Camille. I know it's you."

The three of them, emerging from behind a VW Bug, were red as pomegranates, laughing so hard Kiki thought Jasmine might collapse.

"How nice to see you, ladies," Kiki said, making her friends laugh even harder. "Enjoying the show?"

"The show hasn't even started," Jasmine gasped between giggles. "We were going to wait for you to make out, but we didn't think you would get it on in the parking lot."

"Very mature, Jazz. Thanks." Kiki rolled her eyes at Jacob, making a face, but he didn't smile down at her. Instead, he glared at the Pussycats, giving them the same look that the old man in the Cadillac had given Kiki and Jacob earlier, then he turned and stomped off.

"Are you guys done?" Kiki asked her friends.

"We didn't come here to spy," Sasha insisted. "We just wanted to catch the show. We didn't expect you and Jacob to be out here."

"Could you please, please find someplace else to go?"

"Sure, sure," Camille said, grabbing Jasmine's elbow firmly. "We're out of here."

"Look, I'm sorry," Kiki said when she caught up with Jacob just outside the front door. She dragged him around to the side of the building—there was no need for every trip-hop fan in Nashville to witness this scene. "They can get a little silly."

"A little silly? Those girls don't have the sense of a dumb kitten."

"Those are my friends you're talking about, and they're not stupid. They just like to have fun."

"That's it—fun is everything to them."

Kiki stood as tall as she could, since she was half a foot shorter than Jacob, and put her hands on her hips.

"What's wrong with having fun? What else are they supposed to be doing?"

He laughed at her. It was the first time Kiki had heard him laugh since grade school, but she was not amused.

Jacob shook his head, as if he felt sorry for her friends. "There're all kinds of things they could be doing. But all they do is take up space."

"Well, they're my best friends, so I guess I'm just taking up space too."

Kiki spun and tried to march away, but Jacob grabbed a belt loop and hung on.

"You're different. You're special. And you know it." He was purring right into her ear, but that didn't mean she had to listen.

"Because I know how to hit a drum and think up words that rhyme? In this town everyone and their brother can do that. Let go of me!"

"You know as well as I do that there's a world of difference between you and those girlfriends of yours, and not because your skin is brown either. You're an artist. You can see things they don't see, and understand things they can't even imagine."

Kiki shut her eyes. That struck a chord. She knew her friends had no idea how it felt to come up with just the right words to reduce a feeling to a rhyme, or to have the power to make crowds scream your name. But she wasn't going to let Jacob win this one.

"What makes you think you know what I can and can't see?"

"I know because I see it, too, in every song you ever wrote. I know it because I know you. Your friends can't even tell which songs are yours from listening to the lyrics, can they? They have no idea what's really going on inside you."

Part of Kiki wanted to defend her friends. Part of her wanted to scream at Jacob for imagining that he understood her when they'd had all of one conversation in the last two hours. And part of her couldn't ignore the truth in what he said, that the Pussycats had no idea what was going on inside her—even Mark didn't really understand the first thing about her feelings. And, beneath all her thoughts about friendship and understanding and loyalty and love, Kiki could not ignore Jacob's breath on her neck, or the way his thumb was pressing into the small of her back, an inch away from the black lace edging her thong.

"What makes you think you understand the first thing about me?" she asked, turning back toward him. She meant to stare him down. Instead, she found herself drowning in twin pools of gold, as Jacob stared at her as if she were the only woman left in a world of shadows. This was passion. It had nothing to do with the friendly hookups Kiki had shared with Jason, or the slow-burning tenderness she felt for Mark. Jacob was looking at Kiki as if she was the light after a year of darkness.

Inside, the final band had taken the stage, and the Maze thudded with relentless bass. Kiki leaned against the rough wall and shut her eyes, trying to remember that she wasn't sure what she thought about Jacob. But despite the conflict in her mind, her body didn't mind at all when Jacob leaned in to whisper, "I am part of the beat. I am the dark and the heat. The pulse in your wrist. The dance in your feet. A shot of musical whiskey served up neat."

Kiki felt dizzy, almost drunk: pressed between Jacob's heat and the cold wall, Kiki wasn't thinking at all, her mind awash in sensations as he kissed her. His stubble burned her cheeks and chin, but his lips were soft and insistent. She almost didn't recognize the pulse of her cell phone in her back pocket.

She broke off the kiss and said, "I've got to go home."

"You don't have to do anything you don't want to do," he murmured, leaning in to kiss her again.

She gave him a firm shove. "Seriously. I have to go home."

He gave her the golden stare again, but she resisted this time. She had too much to lose to risk missing her curfew.

"Okay. If that's what you want."

Without another word, he headed for his car. Kiki followed him, still feeling more than a little shaken. The ride home was silent, except for the wind roaring in Kiki's ears. Once they got to her house, he kissed her again, and she had to tear herself away. She climbed out of the car quickly. It was too easy to lose herself in his passion, and her curfew was just minutes away.

"Can I see you tomorrow?" he asked her, his eyes catching the light from the dashboard.

"I'll be in the studio until ten forty-five, and I told Laura Keller I would go to her party." She almost asked if he was going, then remembered that Jacob never went to Wentworth parties. He even skipped their Sophomore Soirée, though there were girls who would have cut off their little fingers to go with him.

"Catch you there."

"Really?" Kiki was trying not to sound shocked, but she was.

He nodded once, as if it was no big deal, then roared off into the quiet streets of Belle Meade.

Kiki was not surprised when her phone rang ten minutes later. The Pussycat Posse knew her curfew very well.

"Yes, Camille?" she answered, wriggling out of her jeans with the phone tucked between her shoulder and her ear.

"Dude, I cannot believe what a dick Jacob was. What's his issue?"

"Well, you guys were being complete idiots," Kiki reminded her. "Come on! We were on a date!"

"What kind of baby just stomps off and has a temper tantrum?"

"What kind of baby walks around singing that stupid song? How old are we, Cam?"

"But we've known each other forever. It's no big deal, singing a song. How much did it bother you?" Camille asked her.

"I wasn't happy about it, for the record. I mean, he'd only just started talking to me. Really talking."

"And you guys went out at seven?" Camille asked. "That's a little weird."

"Seven-thirty. And I think he's a little shy," Kiki admitted. It was strange, thinking of someone like Jacob as shy, but what else would you call someone uncomfortable talking with people, no matter what he'd said about Holden and Jane in *Catcher in the Rye?*

"If he's your soul mate, he can't be shy. You're not shy. You're the opposite of shy," Camille insisted.

"The word is 'extroverted,' and I don't see what that has to do with anything."

"Kiki, he doesn't talk. He flips out over nothing. He's a creep. I know the packaging is nice, but we can totally find you something better."

"You don't know anything about him, Cam."

"And don't you think that's a little weird? I mean, we've been going to school with him for eleven years. I think you should drop him."

Kiki had finished undressing and had shrugged on an old Pink Floyd T-shirt by then, but Camille's suggestion put all thought of sleep out of her mind. Camille gave everyone a chance—well, everyone but Franklin, and only because Kiki had told her exactly how slutty he really was. If anything, Kiki thought Camille was a little too open-minded when it came to guys, and she had a lot more dating experience than Kiki.

On the other hand, Camille hadn't talked to Jacob in years. Kiki had. And a lot of what he said made sense to her. Maybe Camille knew less about Kiki than Jacob did.

"Random change of subject," Kiki said. "Do you know which songs I wrote on *Sorry, We're Open?*"

"Um . . . the third one, 'Carry On'?" Camille guessed.

"'Carry On' is track six. Track three is 'Temptationland.'"

"Did you write that one?" Camille asked.

"'Temptationland' is about getting a blow job, Cam. I didn't write that one."

"Oh. Maybe 'Candy Cigarette'? Why? What's with the Temporary Insanity trivia?"

"Never mind," Kiki said, shaking her head. "I've got to get some sleep."

But once Kiki slid under the covers, she had a hard time falling asleep. Was Camille right about Jacob? Was Jacob right about her? Did it matter, when the thought of his eyes, his hands, his mouth was enough to make the room spin?

SHOULD KIKI TRY HIM ON?
Turn to page 141 to see if Jacob's her perfect fit.

♥

SHOULD KIKI PUT HIM BACK ON THE RACK?
Turn to page 149 to see what happens if she tells him goodbye.

Think it's time Kiki played with fire? Read on to see if Kiki's love life turns red hot or if she just gets burned.

✳ Chapter 5 ✳

Panic at the Disco

"**N**eed a ride to Laura's?" Mark asked when they wrapped their session at the studio the following night.

"No, I've got one." Kiki busied herself wiping down her drums so that she wouldn't have to meet Mark's eyes.

"Who?"

"Jacob."

"You and Young, huh?" Franklin asked, his voice rich with curiosity. "I always thought he was kind of weird."

"He's just quiet," Kiki said, trying not to slam the door as she flew from the recording booth.

Jacob was waiting for her outside, and she didn't wait to watch the studio assistants load her drum kit into Franklin's van. She kissed Jacob hello, but briefly, not wanting to put on a show for the sound engineers and producers gathering outside the studio—not to mention her bandmates.

"So, are you and Laura tight?" Jacob asked while he was stopped at a red light.

"Not really, no." Laura was the only other girl in third period AP Physics. Kiki always worked with her when she and Mark were having a fight.

He snorted, and before Kiki could ask him what his problem was with Laura Keller, the light changed and they screeched off, the rushing winds again so loud that conversation was impossible. The next time they were stopped, though, she returned to the subject.

"You can't say that Laura's dumb. She's probably going to be the valedictorian."

"She's like a diamond-studded calculator: she's pretty, and she crunches numbers, but there's nothing going on inside. Have you ever heard her talk? 'Oh, I can't eat another doughnut. Oh, I look so fat.' She may be book-smart, but she's as shallow as a dirty ditch."

Kiki didn't want to laugh, since Laura really was a sweet girl, but Jacob's imitation of her couldn't have been better.

"So is there anyone in our class you actually like?"

He grinned. "I like you."

"I kind of figured that much. But is there anyone else?"

He shrugged and gunned the engine, pinning Kiki to her seat. It was the last chance they had to talk before they arrived at Laura Keller's house. Both of Laura's parents worked in the music industry, and they were still in New York, but the party was still mostly confined to the basement rec room. It spilled out onto the back lawn, though, where the people who were so drunk they didn't feel the autumn bite in the night air danced to '80s rock, heavy with synth.

"Feel like dancing?" Kiki asked hopefully, as "Take on Me" came on just as they entered the basement.

Jacob made a face, but he took both her hands and began to rock out, old-school. Kiki could sense the stares, even though it was dark enough in the basement that she couldn't see much except other dancing shadows and the drops of light shed by a spinning disco ball. Most people there had to be amazed that Jacob Young had come to a party; others were probably shocked that he had come to a party with Kiki Kelvin. Franklin and Mark were surprised—she could see them watching her from the room's one well-lit corner, by the stereo and the kegs.

And Kiki knew her classmates had to be amazed at how well Jacob danced—she almost wished she could just sit and watch him. Almost, but not quite, especially when the syrupy theme from "Dirty Dancing" came on. Jacob held her so close she thought he would never let her go. She rested her head on his shoulder, thinking how lucky she was to have found someone who was so crazy about her that he would waltz to a song as cheesy as "I've Had the Time of My Life," surrounded by people he couldn't stand, just to be with her.

The next song was one Temporary Insanity covered, "Eternal Flame," by the Bangles.

"Your version is a lot better," Jacob told Kiki, spinning her once before she nestled back in his arms again.

"So you were at the show last week?" It was their first public performance of the song, though they had practiced it, on and off, for a year.

Jacob didn't say anything. Kiki shouldn't have been surprised—after all, he wasn't the most talkative boy she had ever dated—but there was something about this silence that tipped her off.

"You taped the show, didn't you?" She froze in his arms,

then stepped away. "That's why you know the lyrics to 'Welcome to the Dance Floor'—you have a bootleg recording of it."

"It wasn't me," Jacob said instantly. "I wasn't even at the show. I swear."

"Why should I believe you?"

"Have you ever seen me at a show?"

Kiki paused, trying to remember if she had ever seen him, or if anyone had ever mentioned seeing him at a Temporary Insanity show. She couldn't, though. Not once. That's why she was so surprised to see her lyrics on his HelloHello profile.

"But you know someone who did tape it. Care to share, Jacob? Because my label would be very interested in that information. Did they play it over the school PA system instead of the announcements, too, or was that you?"

He didn't answer her—surprise, surprise. He just shoved his hands in his pockets and stared at her with his usual superior expression.

"Franklin!" she shouted at full volume. "Mark! A little help?"

The whispered conversations surrounding the dance floor died, and some of the kids in the backyard came rushing back, sensing a scene about to unfold. Kiki had a singer's lungs, and she could scream very, very loudly.

"That wasn't me!" Jacob insisted.

"Oh really? Why should I believe that?"

"Because we understand each other!"

"Do you understand that taping a live show is illegal?" Kiki's voice rose again to a shout.

Before Jacob could answer, there was a sudden roiling in the crowd.

"What was that?" Franklin demanded, stumbling toward the two of them, clearly trashed. "Is Jacob bootlegging?"

"I think he might be the one who put us on the morning announcements," Kiki said.

"Prove it," Jacob said coldly, crossing his arms.

Franklin just smiled. "Here's proof!" He nailed Jacob in the jaw before Kiki realized what he was doing.

Jacob didn't go down. Instead, he swung at Franklin, only missing because Franklin was so drunk he couldn't stand without weaving. That didn't stop Franklin from landing a punch in Jacob's gut.

"That's enough!" Mark yelled, fighting his way through the crowd to grab Franklin. Kiki had to stand between them and Jacob, who was still trying to land another punch.

"Get lost," Kiki told Jacob. "It's over."

"I'm not finished with him!" Jacob growled.

"I'm finished with you." Kiki turned her back on Jacob and helped Mark drag Franklin to a bathroom upstairs. He struggled all the way, but once they arrived, Franklin slumped thankfully by the toilet and began to hurl.

"This reminds me of our first show in Athens," Mark said cheerfully, sitting on the edge of the tub. Kiki wondered if he was happy because they had someone to blame for the morning announcements prank or because she was clearly single again. "I thought that bouncer was going to kill Franklin."

"Just like old times." Kiki tried and failed to sound as happy as Mark. She slumped next to him, and he gave her a friendly pat on the knee.

"Cheer up, K. You found out who pulled the announcements stunt. You're a hero!"

"A hero who just had the worst date ever!"

"Oh, I can top that. Did I ever tell you about my last date with Sarah Jane?"

Franklin pulled his head out of the toilet and asked, "Did it end with having to take her to a dentist to get out the condom stuck in her braces?"

"Um, no."

"Then it wasn't the worst date ever."

Franklin's head disappeared into the toilet bowl again.

Now Kiki had to laugh. "Thanks, guys. Actually, that does make me feel a little better."

"Yeah, forget that weirdo," Franklin rumbled from inside the bowl. "What do you need with other guys when you've got us?"

Kiki patted him on the back. "I'll try to keep that in mind."

Just then, Camille's tousled blond head popped into the doorway. "When I heard you and Mark were in the bathroom, this is not what I expected."

"Where have you been?" Kiki asked. "You missed all the excitement."

"My timing sucks," she admitted, poking her head a little farther into the room. "Like, I probably shouldn't be here now, but I wanted to make sure you're okay."

"I'm fine," Kiki insisted, her heart squeezing to hear the concern in Camille's voice. Anyone else would have come to say "I told you so." Only a true friend would care more about Kiki's feelings than being right. And even if she and Camille were very different, Camille was a great friend. No matter how Jacob had momentarily twisted Kiki's thinking. "And you can come in. Nothing's happening here."

"Nothing?" Camille asked, full of hope for Kiki and Mark.

"Nothing," Kiki and Mark said at once. Kiki thought she heard something very final in Mark's voice. He might have been jealous of Jacob, but he still wasn't ready to ask Kiki out himself. A week before, Kiki would have been crushed. A day before, she would not have cared either way. But at this moment, she was almost relieved. She wasn't in the mood for going out with anyone just yet, no matter how well she thought she understood him.

"Scoot over," Camille said, edging Kiki and Mark closer together. "I want to hear all about the drama."

"I was a total hero, Camille!" Franklin said. Then he threw up again. Everyone tried to muffle the laughter they couldn't quite contain.

"Franklin was awesome," Kiki said, rolling her eyes at Camille, setting her off again. "Let me tell you all about it."

Sounds like Kiki is tired of boy shopping—are you? Turn to page 149 to see what would have happened if Kiki had dumped Jacob after one date, or turn to page 57 to choose another boy.

Think Kiki should listen to Camille, even if Camille doesn't listen to Kiki's music as much as Jacob does? Read on to see what happens!

✳ Chapter 5 ✳

Breaking Up Is Hard to Do

Kiki hadn't been to Jacob Young's house since his eighth birthday party. It hadn't changed much: it was still elegant and opulent without being gaudy—there was lots of polished wood, and African sculptures on pedestals. Mrs. Young hadn't changed much either. Either she'd had a lot of plastic surgery, or she had very, very good genes.

"Hey, Kiki. What are you doing here?" she asked, squinting down at Kiki at the front door. Kiki had decided to bike over to Jacob's house to tell him in person that she wasn't interested in going out with him again. She had known him so long, surely she owed him that much, even after just one date? Unfortunately that Saturday, like most Saturdays, Kiki had things to do all afternoon. And that night she was going to the studio, and then on to Laura Keller's party, so her best chance for seeing him was at 10:30 AM.

"I need to talk to Jacob. Is he around?" She shifted her backpack nervously from shoulder to shoulder. It hadn't occurred to her that he might be out—like a normal person might be on a Saturday.

"I sent him to the store to pick up some milk. Would you like to wait for him?"

"Sure. That would be great."

Kiki trailed after Mrs. Young, through halls covered with gold records and recessed cases full of awards statuettes.

"Would you like to wait in his room? You two are so close these days, I'm sure he won't mind." Mrs. Young gave Kiki a dazzling smile, which Kiki tried to return. She didn't think Mrs. Young had it in her to be sarcastic, but Kiki could not imagine where Jacob's mother got the idea that she and Jacob were good friends.

She didn't ask directions, of course. She just headed upstairs to Jacob's bedroom. It hadn't moved, but it looked completely different now. Not surprisingly, since there weren't too many high school juniors with race-car beds and NASCAR posters. It was cleaner than most of the boys' bedrooms Kiki had seen, a lot cleaner than Franklin and Mark's rooms, though there was more musical equipment in Jacob's room than in her two bandmates' rooms put together. It was a functioning recording studio, with everything but a glassed-in booth. Knowing whose son Jacob was, that didn't surprise Kiki much. The number of Temporary Insanity posters—four—was a bit of a shock, though.

Even spookier was the stack of music magazines by Jacob's desk. Not that there was anything necessarily weird about music magazines—Kiki had plenty of her own. The same ones, in fact—including a few from Europe and Australia, which she got only because they included interviews with her. She picked up the April issue of *Sound Check*, out of New Zealand, and found the Temporary Insanity interview, dog-eared. Jacob had underlined the parts where she talked about vegetarianism, and something she said about her favorite children's book, *Watership Down*.

"Creepy," Kiki murmured to herself, feeling the hairs on the back of her neck rise. For all she knew, there were hundreds of bedrooms across the US that looked exactly like this. The message boards on the Temporary Insanity website were full of discussions about some little thing she had said in an interview she had forgotten all about, and she had seen the sales figures for her band's posters. But she had never been in a fan's room before, and she wasn't sure where to draw the line between fan and stalker.

She put the magazine away and tried to shake off her shivery mood. She already knew that Jacob was maybe a little obsessed—his knowledge of her music was what had attracted her in the first place. And it didn't really matter, since she didn't plan on talking to him ever again anyway.

She hoped she wouldn't have to wait too long. She had to get back in time for practice—if it was still on. Franklin had talked about canceling.

Kiki turned to Jacob's computer, a sleek new laptop that would have wowed the sound engineers at her favorite studio. Mark was going to e-mail her that morning to confirm the session. She spent enough time around guys to know not to open any of the JPGS saved to the desktop, but she couldn't resist the MP3 named *tempins10/11*.

The drum solo at the beginning of "Friday Night Special" poured out of half a dozen speakers. Her jaw dropped. She didn't have to listen to more than a couple of seconds to recognize the recording that had played over the morning announcements. It was a beautifully mixed bootleg, and one her label would love to hear all about.

As Kiki scrolled through the files, heart pounding, she found another surprise: a recording of the RGB Up-and-Coming show they had played the night of the MTV Video Music Awards. She remembered the date because she and Franklin were glued to the TV whenever they weren't onstage. And Kiki knew that Jacob had been in LA that night with his parents, which supported the rumor that he really was in *Hustle and Flow*. That meant Jacob could have made some of the bootleg recordings, but not all of them. Kiki had the feeling that, short of torture, Jacob would never tell who else was involved—he didn't say much under any circumstances. But Kiki was going to get the truth, no matter what.

Vengeance wasn't Kiki's thing—usually. But this went too far. As far as Kiki was concerned, bootlegging was theft, even if it was all too common. But what really set Kiki off was that Jacob knew every single member of Temporary Insanity. Had known them for years! He wasn't stealing from random strangers—he was stealing from people he saw every day. He was stealing from her, the girl he thought he knew everything about! He actually had the nerve to make out with her, knowing that he was snatching her royalties!

She slipped Jacob's laptop into her backpack and sailed out the bedroom door. She could drop it off at her lawyer's place on the way to the studio.

"Leaving already?" Mrs. Young asked before Kiki could escape. "I'm sure Jacob will be back in a couple of minutes."

"Yeah, something came up. I'll talk to him later. Bye!" The doorknob twisted in Kiki's hand. She had to step back as the door swung open and Jacob backed in, one arm filled with groceries.

"Hi, Jacob. It's over." Kiki skipped out the door.

"WHAT?" both Youngs blurted behind her.

Kiki turned and saw them staring at her with identically wide golden eyes.

"I'll say it again, Jacob, slowly this time, so pay attention. One. Our lawyers are going to call about your illegal Temporary Insanity recordings, so get ready. Two. Consider yourself dumped."

Kiki hefted the backpack to her shoulders and climbed on her bike.

"Wait!" Jacob begged, following her out the door. "I thought—you and I—we have something special! What happened? I don't understand!"

"No, you don't understand anything," Kiki said over her shoulder. "But now I understand you."

"You can't prove anything!" he yelled as she pedaled off.

"Wanna bet?"

Kiki expected to hear him cursing. Instead she heard a strange squelching sound. She glanced over her shoulder to see that Jacob had dropped his groceries and was racing to his car. The way he drove, he would catch up with her long before she got anywhere near her house. He was weird enough when he thought they were soul mates—she didn't want to find out what he would do if he caught up to her now.

If she stuck to the streets, she didn't have a chance. But if she left the streets, sooner or later she'd find herself trying to get her bicycle over someone's security fence. Camille's house was a little closer than her own. She ditched her bike by someone's garage and started running through the gorgeous, well-maintained lawns of Belle Meade.

Kiki's heart thudded in her ears so loud she feared she wouldn't be able to hear Jacob's screeching tires, even if he was right behind her. The thought of all his passion turned to anger was enough to keep her running until she reached Camille's front door, so breathless that it took five minutes to explain to Camille what had happened.

"So you want a ride back to your house?" Camille said, shoving sleep-tangled curls out of her face. She was still in her pajamas—a ratty T-shirt and sweat pants—but she didn't look much different from any other day. There was no sign of a told-you-so sneer on her face. Kiki was so glad to have her as a friend, she almost hugged her. She didn't, when she realized how sweaty she was from her run.

"He's probably waiting there for me, parked across the street."

"Want to call your parents?" Camille suggested.

"No! It would just freak them out."

"Well, what do you want to do? Go to the police station? Call a lawyer?"

"No . . ." Kiki said slowly. "I think I want to call Mark."

"Wow! Do you think he'll be your knight in shining armor?"

Kiki had to laugh at that. "I think he has our best mini-recorder."

Twenty minutes later, they had a plan. They went to work immediately.

"He'll be there," Kiki assured her. Even if Jacob weren't obsessed with her, she had his laptop, and he knew her mother was a judge. There was no way he would think she would just let it slide.

Just as she predicted, Jacob's convertible was parked in front of her house when Mark dropped her off at the curb. She waved goodbye and watched him drive down the street. She started up the driveway, her backpack clutched to her chest, but she stopped when Jacob called her name.

"I already told you it's over," she yelled. "Get lost!"

"You have to let me explain," he said, jogging over. Behind him, Camille's white Volvo was creeping up the street. Mark's battered old car stood out plainly in Kiki's neighborhood, but Camille's car blended in perfectly. She parked in Kiki's neighbor's driveway, a baseball bat cradled in her lap. Kiki wasn't sure that Camille would actually use it, but she trusted her friend to come flying if it actually looked like it might be necessary.

"Jacob, how exactly do you plan to explain seventeen illegal recordings on this computer?" Kiki asked, waving her backpack around for emphasis. Jacob's actual laptop was in Mark's car, on the way to RGB headquarters. But Camille's chemistry book was close enough in size and shape for their plan.

"Well, I . . . well. You know how much I like you." He was standing a good ten feet away from Kiki—too far for the recorder taped inside her bra to pick up his voice. She had to get closer to him, but not too close—she didn't want to give him ideas—or take any chances.

"So you decided to steal my music?" she said, marching right up to him, shaking her backpack threateningly.

"I didn't steal anything," he said. He didn't back off, but he didn't get any closer. "I bought your songs."

"You're saying you bought all of them?"

He sneered. "I don't go to your concerts, Kiki. Most of your fans are bubble-headed idiots. Not that that's your fault. They're all there for Franklin. They have no idea who the real genius is."

Kiki gritted her teeth. "Who from? Who did you buy them from?"

Jacob just looked at her, his arms folded across his chest.

"Jacob, I really will turn this laptop over to the cops, and RGB is going to press charges. People go to jail for stuff like this. If you really are innocent, tell me who's recording our shows."

He just laughed. "You think I care about lawyers? Baby, I care about you! We belong together! I only bought the bootlegs because I wanted to hear every single show I could."

She forced herself not to gag and tried to sound as if she were buying this. "If you really do care about me, Jacob, you'll tell me who sold you the bootlegs."

This time, he didn't even hesitate.

"Katie Fulsome."

"What?"

"Katie Fulsome. Sophomore, wears glasses, complete idiot. She stole this super-high-tech mini-recorder the size of an i-Pod Nano, and she hides it in her bra."

Kiki didn't know what was more surprising: that Katie Fulsome was secretly selling Temporary Insanity bootlegs or that Franklin had been right about something. Katie Fulsome had been his first and only guess at the culprit. It even explained Mark's comment that her bra size changed from concert to concert—she probably had to vary the padding to balance sound distortion in each venue. "You're telling me Katie Fulsome did the recordings?" Kiki said extra-clearly, for the recorder.

"I just said that." Jacob was beginning to sound annoyed. "I've got the e-mails to prove it."

"Really?" Kiki couldn't help grinning. "How interesting."

"Why don't you come back to my place?" he said, grinning back. "I'll show you anything on my computer you want."

"I don't think so," she said, swinging the backpack back to her shoulder. "You should go enjoy your freedom, Jacob, since you're probably going to jail."

"What are you talking about? I just told you that Katie made the recordings, and Katie's the one who hijacked the morning announcements. That has nothing to do with me, with *us*. We've got something special!"

Kiki shook her head in amazement and walked past Jacob, over to Camille's car.

"Where are you going?" he asked, genuinely confused.

"Maybe you're not going to jail. I think you could probably plead insanity, because you have got to be crazy if you think there's anything between us."

"Kiki, wait! We have to talk!"

Kiki didn't even turn around.

"I never thought I'd have to say this, but Jacob Young, you need to shut up. I am sick of hearing your voice."

She got into Camille's car, and they couldn't help but laugh at the sight of Jacob Young still standing in Kiki's driveway, speechless.

Kiki learned more about Jacob after deciding to break up than she might have if she had stayed with him. Turn to page 141 to see how that would have turned out, or to page 57 to pick a new boy.

✽ Chapter 4 ✽

Joshua

The morning after she e-mailed Joshua, Kiki was wondering if she had made the right decision. She loved the way his deep-black hair contrasted with his golden skin, and she didn't mind muscles on a man. On the other hand, even though Joshua might be a little deeper than the average jock, he was still a jock.

"Relax, Kiki," Sasha whispered at the beginning of homeroom. "You like drumsticks and he likes lacrosse sticks. It's a match made in heaven."

Kiki glared at her. "I think I liked you better before you fell in love."

Sasha stuck out her tongue, but before she could respond, Dr. Eckhart said over the intercom, "Good morning, Lions. Today is Tuesday, October 13th, and these are your morning announcements."

For the next few hours, Kiki was busy dashing from class to class, always trying to get as much of her homework done in school as she possibly could. But in study hall, instead of working on her history paper she asked permission to get on the Internet.

"For research purposes?" the librarian, Mrs. Moser, asked.

"Of course." Kiki gave Mrs. Moser her most convincing smile, and after looking up a few random facts about the reign of James I, she checked her email.

From: *jlcheng@southweb.net*
To: *k^3@rgb.com*
Re: Salutations

Hi Kiki,

Thanks for your e-mail. My schedule is also a little crazy right now, but Friday is my good day too—no practice. But I have a game on Saturday afternoon, so I can't stay out too late. Could we get together right after school? I could pick you up. I can't remember if Wentworth has uniforms. If it does, you should probably change into something that you won't mind getting dirty.

Later,
Joshua

Kiki printed out a copy, along with some articles about the English monarchy, and brought Joshua's e-mail to lunch in the Senior Common Room. It was really just a dusty attic space with a few couches rescued from the teacher's lounge, still reeking of cigarettes, but the Pussycat Posse liked to eat lunch up there when they had something private to discuss. No one else ever used it.

She had sworn the Pussycat Posse to secrecy—she didn't want anyone in school to know she was boy shopping online. Especially Mark.

"Not that Mark cares at all whether I'm getting e-mail from random jocks," Kiki said bitterly, slurping up some lo mein while Sasha and Camille reread the e-mail.

"You're supposed to be forgetting about Mark," Jasmine pointed out. She was snooping through the piles of old books stacked at random around the room. "I've never understood what you see in him, anyway. He's so boring and uptight."

"What are you going to say if he actually asks you out?" Kiki asked, hoping to hear another one of Jasmine's patented put-downs.

Jasmine's eyes narrowed. "Yes."

"What?" screeched everyone else.

Jasmine slammed down the elderly textbook she held and rolled her eyes. "Come on, people. We've all been trying to figure out what's going on in Mark's head for the last three years. If he asked me out, of course I would say yes. Not because I like him—" She made a quick gagging motion. "I think he's a dork. But I wouldn't mind a chance to pick his brain."

"Do me a favor," Kiki said slowly. "If he asks you out, just say no. Okay?"

"Well, sure." Jasmine shrugged. "I still don't think he'll actually do it."

"You never know what he's thinking," Kiki said unhappily.

"Unlike this Josh guy," Jasmine said, plopping down next

to Kiki on a couch. It sent up a cloud of dust in protest. "Jocks are about as hard to understand as Jell-O pudding."

"Huh?" Camille asked. "What do you know about pudding?"

"I don't agree," Sasha said, heading off what threatened to be a completely pointless discussion about instant desserts. "Just because Josh likes sports doesn't mean he's brainless. Thomas is really into cricket, and he's—"

Sasha ducked to avoid three dusty pillows sailing her way.

"Yes, Sasha, we know exactly how smart, and charming, and sweet Thomas is," Camille said wearily. "You've already told us all about it."

"I was just saying that just because Joshua likes sports doesn't mean he's dumb." Seeing the disbelieving look on Kiki's face, Sasha changed the subject. "What do you think he has in mind for your first date? Hiking? A picnic, maybe? That would be romantic."

Kiki chewed on a dreadlock nervously. "He's probably going to try to teach me how to play lacrosse."

Jasmine sniggered. "That ought to be pretty funny. Remember when Coach Peter tried to teach field hockey in gym? You managed to bruise his ankle and give him a black eye!"

"Ha ha."

"Just relax and see what happens," Sasha advised, still shaking dust out of her hair from the thrown pillows. "Maybe Joshua will surprise you."

He did. He showed up at Wentworth on Friday afternoon, looking just as good as he did in his picture. His hair had grown since the photo was taken, a dark curtain shading his eyes, and his teeth were an almost fluorescent white against his golden skin. He looked like he belonged on the cover of a health class textbook.

Instead of a lacrosse shirt, he was wearing a black thermal undershirt, shredded jeans, and a tool belt, weighted down with tools that Kiki could not even name, except for the hammer.

"Car trouble?" Kiki asked, joining him inside his neat little Camry.

He laughed, a nice, quiet laugh, not at all like the hooting Kiki associated with the boys of Wentworth football. But Joshua's school, Kenwood, was even preppier than Wentworth, and lacrosse a little more refined than football. Or so she guessed; she really didn't know much about it.

"You don't know much about cars, huh?" he said, starting his up.

"Absolutely nothing."

"Automotive maintenance 101: this is a hammer, and you don't want to use it on much of anything inside a car."

"I'll try to remember that," Kiki said, watching Wentworth shrink in the rearview mirror. The Pussycat Posse had wanted to see her off, but she had promised a slow, horrible death to anyone who spied.

"I guess you don't have much experience with construction either?"

Kiki tried to keep from grimacing. She was a seventeen-year-old girl. Why would she know anything about construction?

He interpreted her annoyance as fear. "Don't worry," he said, patting her knee. "It's not that hard."

"Why would I be worried about construction?" she couldn't help asking.

"'Cause we're going to build a house."

After waiting a minute to see if he was going to burst out laughing, Kiki said, "I don't think I understand. Did you say we are going to build a house?"

"Exactly." He grinned. Under any other circumstances, Kiki would have liked his smile. It was confident, but not especially cocky, and he had dimples. But at that point she was trying to decide whether or not he was a lunatic, and the smile didn't help.

"I thought you said that you had to get home early tonight. I'm pretty sure it takes more than seven or eight hours to build a house."

"It does. But people have been working on it all day."

"Okay, okay, I give up," Kiki said, holding up both hands in surrender. "I have no idea what you're talking about."

It turned out that Joshua volunteered once a month with Habitat for Humanity, a group that builds homes for people who cannot afford to buy them on their own. By the time Kiki and Joshua arrived, the frame was up, the roof was done, and the walls were beginning to look like walls. People cheered when Joshua showed up, since it turned out he was especially good at wiring. The volunteers welcomed Kiki too, even though she had never swung a hammer and thought that a screwdriver was something made with vodka and orange juice.

Kiki spent most of the afternoon bringing people plastic cups filled with Gatorade, though Joshua showed her how a fuse box really worked, and the basics of running electricity through a house. Kiki was impressed, not just that he knew how to do this, but that he wanted to. She gave plenty of clothing to the Salvation Army, played charity concerts, and donated cans to the yearly Wentworth food drive, but volunteer work had never been a part of her life. She was just too busy.

When she admitted that to Joshua, who was carefully screwing a wall socket into place, he just shrugged.

"If something matters to you, you make time for it."

Kiki couldn't argue with that. She started to slink away, feeling embarrassed, but he caught her hand.

"You can't do everything all the time, though," he continued. "Some months I spend eight hours a week tutoring immigrants in English and sixteen doing stuff like this. Other times, I only do eight hours a month. Then I feel bad, because people like Phil—" He waved at a man installing the front door, who waved back. "Phil does some form of volunteer work thirty hours a week. It's like another full-time job, and Phil's a banker, which keeps him pretty busy. You just have to do whatever feels right for you, right now."

"Thanks." Kiki smiled shyly. "My schedule is really crazy at the moment."

"Tell me about it." Josh rolled his eyes. "Could you hand me a few more screws?"

By the time the sun went down, tremendous progress had been made toward completing the house. Kiki was amazed that so much could happen in one day.

"Teamwork," Josh said, throwing an arm around her shoulders. "It's an amazing thing."

The volunteers went to dinner at a nearby spaghetti place. The family who would be moving into the new house was there, a Vietnamese family that had moved to New Orleans just a year before Hurricane Katrina hit: a shy father, sniffling mother, and three adorable kids who ran around asking everyone what color their new rooms were going to be. Kiki was afraid that she would be left out, since everyone else seemed to know each other so well, but Joshua never stopped talking to her. He even tried to show her the rules and strategies of lacrosse with salt and pepper shakers, silverware, and one of his meatballs.

He dropped Kiki off at Camille's house at 7:30, where the girls were gathering before going together to the Trip-Hop Triple Threat at the Maze. He gave her a kiss goodbye, which began as a gentle brush of lips and ended with caressing tongues, though he didn't try to caress anything else.

Kiki was so happy when she came in, Jasmine asked if she was high.

"High on life," Kiki squealed, giving one of Camille's ridiculous heart-shaped pillows a hug. "High on love!"

"And what about Mark?" Jasmine asked with one raised eyebrow. "I'm pretty sure he's going to be at the Maze tonight."

Kiki was so giddy she didn't even wonder why Jasmine would know something like that. "Mark who?"

Two hours later at the Maze, when Kiki heard the insistent beep of an incoming text message, she didn't feel the usual flip-flop of her heart, accompanied by the inevitable question: is it Mark? But her heart soared when she saw that it was, in fact, Joshua, inviting her to his tournament the next day, beginning at 8:00 AM.

She responded instantly, with her regrets: she was dying to see him, but not that early. If he made it to the finals, maybe she would make it then.

No worries. Will b in finals. C u @ 2.

"Wow," Jasmine said, peering over Kiki's shoulder. "Pretty cocky, huh?"

"He's just self-confident. He knows he's good—why should he pretend he doesn't?"

Camille, Jasmine, and Sasha all burst out laughing, making everyone else in line to get into the club stare at them.

"What?"

"It's nothing," Sasha said, still laughing. "It's just that—"

"It's just that Joshua sounds a lot like you," Jasmine finished. "A lot more than seventy-seven percent compatible."

Kiki couldn't say it wasn't true—she did know her strengths, and she didn't see a reason to pretend otherwise. So she just tossed her hair over her shoulder like Franklin did when he was feeling especially arrogant and said, "You guys are ridiculous."

"I know you are but what am I?" Camille giggled.

"If you don't get yourselves under control, I won't take you to the tournament with me."

It was an empty threat, but it kept the teasing to a minimum for the rest of the night. And that was the best Kiki could hope for.

* Chapter 5 *
In the Pink

In the end, only Camille came with Kiki to the lacrosse tournament. This wasn't a big surprise for Kiki—Jasmine and
Sasha's black lace and high heels would have been out of place
in the stands. Even Kiki had chosen blue jeans and sneakers
to wear with her black sweater. Camille was wearing her usual
uniform of jeans and a T-shirt. She blended in perfectly in the
stands packed with fans, most of them dead silent, completely
focused on the game. The two girls sitting in front of Kiki were
the exception, whispering nonstop.

Kiki ignored them at first, looking for Josh. It was easy to
pick him out, since his golden skin glowed in sharp contrast
to his white uniform. He was almost dancing across the field,
as if he were seeing the whole game from above, like a spec-
tator in the stands. Even if Kiki didn't entirely understand all
the rules, she could see that he approached lacrosse the same
way she approached music: when he was on the field, his whole
universe was the game. And that impressed her almost as much
as his dedication to volunteer work. She had finally found a

guy outside of the music world who could understand her devotion to it. She was beginning to think she might be in love.

Soon Kiki realized that the whispering girls in front of her were following Josh's every move too, on and off the field. She elbowed Camille, mimed zipping her lips, then pointed to the two girls.

"I heard on Friday that Jessica wants to get back together with him, but he says he's totally done with the girls here. He thinks we're all boring," one of the girls moaned sadly.

"Where's he going to meet girls? All he does is practice, practice, practice, and do his homework. He's up for the Stillman prize, did you know?"

"I heard someone from Harvard already called guidance about him. Can you believe it? I would die to marry someone like him."

Camille made a face at that, forcing Kiki to cover her mouth with both hands. Her laugh died, though, at the girls' next comment.

"Yeah. If it weren't for the whole getting-arrested-for-selling-heroin thing, Josh Cheng would be absolutely perfect."

Kiki felt her stomach twist. She couldn't have heard right. She looked at Camille.

Camille frowned, then mouthed, "Heroin?" Kiki's stomach twisted harder. She just shook her head. She had no idea what that was about.

Josh's team won the game. He broke away from the crowds flooding the field, taking the stands two at a time to reach Kiki. He swooped down for a quick kiss before she could say anything. When he was done, all thoughts of drugs had completely fled Kiki's mind. It helped that the girls who had been gossiping about him before had joined the other Kenwood fans rushing the field, lost to Kiki's view.

"We're having a victory party tonight, after the official dinner," he said, one sweaty arm still wrapped around Kiki's waist. "You're welcome too," he told Camille.

"I'm actually in the studio until ten-thirty," she said regretfully. And after that she had planned on going to see the Jennifers, or maybe to Laura Keller's party. But the thought of spending more time with Josh was very tempting.

"I can pick you up," Camille said helpfully, bobbing to her feet. "I mean, if the party's still going on by the time we get there."

Josh laughed his quiet laugh. Kiki loved to hear it.

"The party will definitely be going on at eleven. Let me give you the directions."

While he and Camille hashed that out, Kiki's mind went back to the comment about drugs. She could not think of a single way to subtly bring it up, and she couldn't just come out and say, "So, did you sell heroin or what?"

Josh leaned down for a goodbye kiss. Unlike their goodbye from the night before, this one was fast and a little rough— Kiki was as conscious of his hand at the base of her skull as she was of his tongue and teeth. It left her a little breathless, wondering what it would be like to be alone with someone so forceful, especially since his strength was usually so contained. Kiki's mind was still reeling as she and Camille headed over to the recording studio.

"So what do you think?" Kiki asked, after she was once again capable of speech.

"He seems awesome." Camille bubbled with happiness for Kiki, almost as bubbly as Kiki was herself.

"But what about the heroin thing?" Kiki asked, more than a little worried. She knew plenty of kids who smoked pot, and musicians who snorted coke before going onstage, but she didn't know anyone who messed with heroin.

"I'm sure it's just some sort of misunderstanding. Josh doesn't seem like the kind of guy who would smoke pot, much less deal heroin. See you tonight," Camille said cheerfully, dropping her off.

Kiki had to spend the first five minutes of their studio time hiding in the bathroom, doing breathing exercises to clear her mind, which was seesawing wildly from being completely taken by Josh and terrified that he really was a drug dealer. RGB would drop her instantly if they thought she might become a liability—and a boyfriend with a record for heroin possession did not look good in the press. Amazingly enough, her breathing exercises worked. When she walked into the recording booth, put on her headphones and settled in behind the drum kit, Josh and the possible felony record slid right out of her brain, replaced by thoughts of production values and sound quality. Mark and Franklin were already there, also in professional mode. They nodded hello to her, and the three of them had a brief chat with the sound engineers, producers, and both of their managers on the other side of the glass. Then they rocked out, studio-style, for the next few hours.

Once 10:30 rolled around, they wrapped the session. There were smiles all around, especially on the faces of Frederick and Charlie, their managers. While they packed up, Charlie asked, "So what are you kids up to tonight?"

"Party in Belle Meade," Franklin said. "How about you guys?"

"I think I'll go over to Laura's," Mark said, glancing at Kiki from beneath his long, dark lashes. "At least for a little while."

"Not me," Kiki said cheerfully.

"Where are you off to?" Mark asked, his voice a little too sharp. Kiki was still high from the intense session, and the thought of spending more time with Josh was more than enough to take away the sting in Mark's tone.

"I'm going to a lacrosse party. Kenwood Prep lacrosse," she told him, tucking her drumsticks into her back pocket. She pretended not to see Mark and Franklin's identically shocked faces, or Frederick and Charlie's identically amused expressions. "See ya!"

Camille was already waiting when Kiki skipped down the studio stairs, giggling a little at what had sounded suspiciously like jealousy from Mark. How like him, Kiki thought, to decide he likes me just when I decide I like somebody else more.

"You want to stop by your house to change?" Camille asked her.

"Just stop at a Starbucks; I'll change in the bathroom. You look great, by the way." She really did. Camille had traded her usual jeans and T-shirt for a baby-blue sweater that hugged her curves, and a flouncy white skirt that showed off her long legs.

Camille giggled. "Since this is a jock party, I went for the cheerleader look."

"You are so silly," Kiki sighed.

"True. But I look good!"

"Now who's cocky?"

"I just know my strengths, Miss Missy, just like you."

Kiki wasn't sure that her outfit actually showed her own strengths, at least the physical ones. She had chosen black jeans and a blood red sweater with a deep V-neck for the evening, along with a pair of black kitten heels. It was the closest thing to preppy clothes that she owned. She didn't think there was much chance that she would fit in with Josh's friends, but this was the best she could do.

Kiki sent Josh a text message when they left the studio, so he was waiting in front of the massive white clapboard farmhouse, rattling with Justin Timberlake's "SexyBack," when the girls arrived. Joshua gave Kiki a hello kiss that rattled her to her bones. She would much rather spend the evening getting to know Josh a little better in the back of his car, but he wanted her to meet his friends. They walked arm in arm, with Camille on Kiki's other side, up the long drive to the house.

Kiki never went to Wentworth jock parties, but she imagined that they were a lot like the Kenwood lacrosse victory party. Plenty of hot, preppy boys drinking beer, playing poker, and making out with cheerleader types. Someone called Carter was doing a keg stand in the middle of what looked like a living room when Kiki walked in. A guy holding one of Carter's legs dropped it when he saw Camille. One look at her long, bare legs and Carter wound up lying in a puddle of spilled beer.

"Hey, everybody," Josh said, stepping over Carter to get to a stack of empty Styrofoam cups. "This is Kiki and Camille. They go to Wentworth."

Everyone wandered over to say hello, except for the girls, who eyed Kiki and Camille with suspicion, and the boys playing cards. Josh handed each of them a can of Bud. Camille downed hers, and Kiki's too, when Josh wasn't looking. Kiki knew there would be some vodka or rum around somewhere, probably in a freezer. But she never even saw the kitchen, because Josh led her to the backyard where more of his friends and teammates were watching a vast bonfire. The conversation wasn't much different from any other party, except that the gossip was all about people Kiki had never met. After twenty minutes of utter boredom, Kiki went looking for Camille, but couldn't find her anywhere. When she got back to the fire, Josh had also disappeared.

"Maybe he's looking for a fix," one of the cheerleader types said when Kiki asked where he had gone. Everyone but Kiki laughed.

One of the players—Kiki thought his name was William— took pity on her. "I think he went to get another drink."

"Thanks!" She headed back to the house and found Josh in the den, doing a keg stand. The crowd had already reached the count of twenty when she crossed the threshold, and he was still going strong. She decided to go look for Camille again, and perhaps the kitchen, when she got drawn into a conversation with some people standing by the stereo.

"Best group ever with a color in their name?" a tall, red-haired girl asked her. It was the first friendly question a girl there had asked her, so Kiki had to answer.

"Pink Floyd."

"Is that what Pink's band is called?" one of the lacrosse boys asked.

"No way!" Kiki wanted to wash his mouth out with soap. "They were one of the most creative rock bands ever. Haven't you ever heard of *The Wall?*"

They shook their heads. The boy who had asked about Pink sneered. "They can't be that good if no one has ever heard of them."

Kiki thought that was one of the stupidest things anyone could ever say. "Music is a business, and a band doesn't necessarily succeed because they're the best. Sometimes it's just because they produce the right sound at the right time. Right as in popular, not right as in good. Pink Floyd was completely ahead of its time in terms of—"

"Hey, Josh," yelled the Pink fan. "Can you come shut your girlfriend up?"

"Show some manners, Reg," Josh said, weaving his way over. "Be polite to the ladies. Now what's your damned problem?"

"She's getting all hot and bothered about some stupid band."

"Pink Floyd is not a stupid band!" Kiki insisted. "They are legendary! Just because you're so ignorant you've never heard of them—"

"Chill, girlfriend," said the redhead. "You need a drink. Is that keg tapped?"

"I don't want a drink," Kiki said, fuming. It would have bothered her less if Josh's friends all hated Pink Floyd rather than the fact that they didn't even know who Pink Floyd was. But even that bothered her less than the way they all seemed to agree that if a band was any good, they would know all about it. That really was ignorant, and it wasn't an attitude Kiki could tolerate very long. "Josh, do you know who Pink Floyd was?"

"Is that Pink's last name?" he asked. "I've heard of her."

"See? Nobody has ever heard of these girls," Reg said.

"Just because you haven't doesn't mean nobody knows who they are. And there were no women in Pink Floyd!"

"What's the big deal?" Josh asked. He looked genuinely confused. "I mean, they're just a band."

"It's not about the band, Josh! It's about being so close-minded that you think you and your friends are the entire world."

"Huh." He nodded, then patted her on the shoulder as if she were a dog that could be soothed by petting. "I'm going to get you a drink."

"Don't bother," Kiki said. "I'm feeling kind of tired. Have you seen my friend Camille?"

"Yeah, but I'm pretty sure she's not going anywhere any time soon." The way the guys all laughed told Kiki what Camille was up to, even if she didn't know who Camille was doing it with. She thought about asking more questions, but trusted that Camille knew what she was doing. She was a big girl, and she always kept plenty of condoms in her purse, just in case.

"Ah. Okay." This night had seriously gone downhill. "And I guess you can't drive right now, huh?"

"I probably could, but there's no way I could pass a Breathalyzer if I got pulled over. Could you wait another hour? Or I could get someone else to drive you home."

"Don't worry about it," she said, pulling out her cell phone. "I'll find a ride."

Josh pulled her aside, well away from his friends. "I'm really sorry. If I had thought you'd want to go home so soon, I wouldn't have done that keg stand."

"No big deal," she said, speed-dialing Jasmine. Her friend didn't pick up. She knew that Sasha was with Thomas somewhere, and wouldn't want to be interrupted. That left her other best friend.

"Hey, Mark. Would you mind coming to get me?"

Kiki expected Mark to make a big deal out of it. He had to know that another boy was involved. Even before his recent weirdness, Mark would have made fun of her for getting stuck like this. But he hadn't had a terribly good time at Laura Keller's, especially after Franklin got puking drunk. Mark had had to watch over him in the bathroom to make sure he didn't drown in the toilet. He was glad to have a good excuse for passing the responsibility for Franklin on to someone else.

"You have any Pink Floyd in the car?" Kiki asked, tilting her seat back.

"Of course. Check the CD case." Kiki slipped *Dark Side of the Moon* into his nice new CD player. It was probably more expensive than the car itself, and the sounds of the world-famous album pouring from the speakers soothed Kiki's jumbled emotions.

"You know they're doing *Dark Side of the Wizard* tomorrow at the Belcourt."

"Hmm?" She had been doing the breathing exercise again, and it had done its job. She wasn't as pissed off at Joshua anymore. The music thing wasn't that big a deal, after all, and even if Josh's friends were idiots, he was still a decent guy. After all, he could have flipped out when Kiki called a guy to come pick her up, but he was perfectly fine about that.

"There are all these weird moments when *Dark Side of the Moon* seems to describe what's going on in *The Wizard of Oz*, if you start the music at the right time. Like when the wicked witch shows up, it's on the line, 'You don't know which is which and who is who.' Stuff like that. It's supposed to be really cool. Franklin and I were talking about going to see it."

"That sounds like fun." She wondered if Josh would like to see it, but he would probably be doing volunteer work.

That's when it hit her: volunteer work was the same thing as community service, which was the punishment Kiki's mom liked to give for underage, first-time offenders. Was Josh doing hundreds of hours of community service because he wanted to, or because he had to? Did Kiki want to go out with someone who might be a criminal?

SHOULD KIKI TRY HIM ON?
Turn to page 181 to see if Joshua's her perfect fit.

❤

SHOULD KIKI PUT HIM BACK ON THE RACK?
Turn to page 189 to see what happens if she tells him goodbye.

✳ *Chapter 6* ✳

Welcome to the Dark Side of the Moon

The next morning—well, early afternoon—when Kiki rolled out of bed, she gave Josh a call.

"How would you like to find out what's so great about Pink Floyd?"

"Sounds good to me," he said cheerfully. "I'm glad you got home all right, even if you didn't dig the party."

"It was okay, I guess, but there is something I have to ask you about. Something someone said at the party." Of course, she'd heard about it long before the party, but she didn't see any reason to tell him that. "Were you arrested for dealing heroin?"

After a long pause he said, "Not exactly."

"How do you 'not exactly' get arrested?"

"I did get arrested, but not because the police thought I had drugs. I got arrested because I was driving home from a party and I realized that the road seemed a lot curvier than it was on the way to the party, so I pulled over to sleep it off. A cop turned up around five in the morning. I had sobered up by then, but apparently you're not supposed to sleep in cars on the side of the road. I got a little angry, because I'd pulled over so I wouldn't endanger anyone, and here's a cop hassling me for that. So then they decided to search the car. They found a bag of creatine powder—I was trying to bulk up—and basically just decided it was heroin. They wound up dropping all the charges, but that was about the worst hangover of my entire life." Josh laughed at the memory.

"So you didn't get sentenced to community service?"

"Of course not. Is that what you thought? That I had to do volunteer work?"

"Well, yeah, I wondered."

"I won't say that I'm only doing it out of the goodness of my heart. I've got some selfish reasons too. I've got my eye on college applications. For the Ivy League, just being good at lacrosse might not be enough. But no one is making me do community service."

Kiki had to laugh. She'd thought he was a criminal, but the worst thing he was guilty of was worrying about college. Two hours after their discussion, she was getting into his car.

"Hey," he said, kissing her hello very chastely on the cheek. When that first kiss turned into a second, sexier one, giving him a taste of her new cake-batter flavored lip gloss, and a third, flavored by the mint he had eaten on the way to pick her up, Kiki broke it off.

"Josh, my mother is weeding the gardenias *right over there*." She jerked her head toward the shadows on the far side of her front porch.

"She isn't watching us."

"Hello," Kiki said firmly, removing his hand from her lap.

"I am not interested in testing that. And we need to leave anyway if we're going to get popcorn."

"All right. Can't blame a guy for trying." He winked at her, and she had to smile back.

But she wasn't smiling later in the movie theater when he started fondling her knee, before Dorothy Gale fell into the pigpen while the movie was still black-and-white.

"Cut it out," she whispered, elbowing him in the ribs. She glared at him to show him she meant it. They arrived late, so that the only seats available were near the front, where everyone could see them by the light reflected of the screen. There was a better-than-even chance that Mark and Franklin were in the crowd somewhere. Kiki had searched in vain for Franklin's platinum head, but that didn't mean that he wasn't there somewhere. And *The Wizard of Oz* was rated G, so there were plenty of kids in the theater, and Kiki was not interested in giving them a show.

Josh sighed and gave up. He slumped in his seat, making the springs creak. He fidgeted with his watch, turning the Indiglo on, then turned his cell phone on. Several people, including Kiki, shushed him when it beeped to let him know that he had messages.

"What?" he whispered back. "I'm bored."

"SHHH!" hissed half a dozen people. He glared over his shoulder before settling back into his seat. Then popcorn began flying in their direction.

"Who's doing that?" Josh shouted, jumping to his feet. "You need to meet me outside, asshole!"

Kiki slid farther down into her seat, wishing she were invisible. Her standards for theater behavior weren't high—

Franklin had been known to throw popcorn once in a while, and she and Mark were terrible about whispering snarky comments during movies. But whispering and goofing around was one thing. Challenging people to fight was a whole new level. And he made no effort to hide how bored he was, even though he knew that Kiki really wanted to be there.

"This is bogus," Josh growled. "I'm outta here." He stood and looked at Kiki. "You coming?"

Kiki shook her head. She didn't want to go anywhere with Josh, now or ever.

He didn't seem surprised—or disappointed.

"Fine. Enjoy your old-ass movie and your weird-ass music." Joshua stomped up the aisle and out of the theater.

Kiki tried to focus again on the movie, but someone plopped into the seat beside her. Mark. Great, she thought. "Here to tell me my date was a complete jerk?" she whispered. "'Cause I already worked that out for myself, thanks."

"Um, no, actually, I was going to apologize. That was me and Franklin throwing the popcorn."

Kiki punched him in the arm, but not as hard as she could. "Why am I not surprised?"

"You know us too well," he said, giving her a one-armed hug. It was the most comfortable moment they had shared since the night he had asked about Jasmine. "Come sit with us."

She followed Mark to the back of the movie theater and settled into her seat. On-screen, Technicolor had just enlivened the world of Oz. Kiki and Mark sat a few rows behind Franklin and his favorite groupie, Lizzie. They were making out energetically. Mark glanced at Kiki, who gave him a little nod. He flicked a piece of popcorn at Franklin's head.

Franklin didn't notice, so Mark threw a few more. The man sitting in a row between him and Franklin didn't seem to mind; he was already shielding his ten-year-old's eyes from Franklin and Lizzie's spectacle. But when a couple of pieces hit Lizzie, it was her turn to jump to her feet.

Mark and Kiki ducked, but it didn't help. Lizzie threw her entire bag of popcorn in their general direction.

"You four: out!" hissed an usher, waving his flashlight at them. They slunk out in embarrassment, Kiki clutching her bucket of popcorn to her chest as if it was a teddy bear. As soon as they hit the pavement outside the Belcourt, the contents of the bucket hit Lizzie and Franklin.

"You guys suck!" Lizzie wailed, running down the street.

"What are you going to do to defend your girlfriend?" Mark teased Franklin, who was red-faced with a combination of anger and amusement. "Challenge us to pistols at dawn?"

"Super Soakers at Jamie's party tonight," Franklin declared. "After practice." He spun on his heel and chased after Lizzie.

"You're on," Kiki called after him. It wouldn't be the first time they had chased each other through the woods with water guns, and it wouldn't be the last. She and Mark wandered up the street, back to his car, their hands not quite touching.

"You know, we really do make a good team," Mark said once they had climbed into the Karmann Ghia.

"Yes, Mark. I do know."

Then, because there would never be a better moment, Kiki kissed him, gently, sweetly, on the lips.

"Why didn't you do that six months ago?" he asked her, pulling away.

"Why didn't you?" She kept her voice light, but her question was serious.

"Because you're my best friend." His eyes were just as serious. "You've got Jasmine and Camille and all. I have Franklin. I couldn't just say, 'Hey, let's get it on.' What if you said no? Everything would be screwed up."

"You don't think things have been more than a little screwed up lately? Like when you asked if Jasmine was free?"

"I was going to ask you out. *Out* out, I mean. But then, when the moment came, I froze. I just asked the first question that came into my mind. I had some idea that Jasmine could tell me whether you were interested, but mostly I was just afraid."

Kiki wanted to be angry with him, but, in the end, it was fear that had kept her from asking him out. Fear that he would reject her, fear that the rejection would kill their friendship. And it cheered her to know that their friendship meant just as much to him as it did to her.

"Good thing one of us is brave, huh?" she said, kissing him again. It didn't turn wild and forceful like Josh's kisses. It was the kiss of two people who knew each other inside and out, slow and lingering and playful, arms wrapped around each other so tight Kiki wondered if they would ever let go.

"I have an idea," Mark whispered, winding a couple of dreadlocks around his fingers. "Let's go over to my house and think up a strategy for killing Franklin later."

Kiki smiled up at Mark. She knew Mark well enough to know that whatever he might say about strategy, he was thinking about something else entirely. "I can't think of anything I would rather do."

This wasn't the happy ending Kiki expected, but she doesn't mind. Want to know what would have happened if Kiki had decided to dump Joshua instead of going to the movie with him? Turn to page 189. To try out another boy, turn to page 57.

* Chapter 6 *

There Is No Dark Side of the Moon

When Kiki finally rolled out of bed the next morning, she checked her cell phone. There was a text from Camille letting her know she'd gotten home all right. Kiki texted back *Me 2*. She frowned at the phone a minute, then she gave Josh a call.

"You know, Josh, I've been thinking, and I don't think we should see each other again. We don't actually have all that much in common."

"Is this just about the music thing? 'Cause I have to say, I think I felt a real connection."

"Of course it's not just about the music." Kiki could date someone who didn't like Pink Floyd—in fact she had, at least twice. Classic rock was not everyone's gig. But Kiki could not imagine dating someone who spent all his time with such mindless losers, the kind of stereotypical prep school kids who gave all the others a bad name. And she didn't appreciate the way he was downing beer while she was left to fend for herself with a bunch of snotty strangers. She wouldn't drag a date to band practice, and didn't appreciate that Josh was unable to find any time during the entire weekend to spend alone with her. And, yeah, there was the whole dealing heroin thing.

"Well, then, I guess I'll see you around. Nice knowing you, Kiki," he said.

"You, too. Good luck with your lacrosse and stuff."

"Yeah. Later."

When the phone rang a little while later, she thought it might be Josh calling her back. Instead it was Mark, asking if she wanted to go to *Dark Side of the Wizard.* Kiki persuaded her mother to leave her gardening chores long enough to drop her off at the Belcourt.

She spotted Franklin, Mark, and Franklin's groupie Lizzie through the glass doors of the movie theater, buying popcorn. She hurried to the ticket-buyers' line and was surprised to find Josh standing near the front. He was slumped in a baggy jacket as if he was afraid someone would recognize him.

"Hey," Kiki said, heading straight for him. "What are you doing here?"

He shrugged, shyly, she thought. "You were so intense about the whole Pink Floyd thing. I saw in the paper that they were doing this, so I decided to see what's so great about them."

Kiki could feel herself blushing. She had assumed that his whole "felt a real connection" thing just meant that he hadn't had a chance to get in her pants yet, and he didn't want to quit seeing her until he had. Maybe they did share a deep connection—she felt like they did—but then she remembered how different they actually were.

"If you want the real Pink Floyd experience, you have to

see *The Wall*." Kiki said. "It's this movie they did—very strange. The soundtrack, though, is completely amazing."

"I've never heard of it," Josh admitted.

"Yes, you have." She sang the "We don't need no education" chorus, which he recognized instantly. It was one of those songs everyone had heard somewhere, even if they didn't know who wrote it.

"What section of the video store is it in?"

"Musicals, probably." She laughed. "At least, I think so." There was a world of difference between the vaginas on legs in *The Wall* and the dance numbers in *Oklahoma!* and *Annie*, but it was mostly music.

"Tell you what," Kiki said, slipping her arm in his. "I have it on DVD. Want to skip this and watch it at my place?"

"Are you sure?" he asked warily.

"Sure I'm sure," she said. "'Watch a movie' is not code for a drunken sexual rampage. I really am inviting you over to watch a movie."

"Cultural education?" he asked.

"Riiiiight."

But once they got in the car, Kiki remembered the whole might-be-a-criminal thing. She wouldn't want to introduce her mother to someone she'd already met in the courthouse.

"So, uh, I heard something weird at the party," she said as they pulled out of the parking lot. "About how you once got busted for heroin?"

He snorted at that. "Yeah, I got busted for heroin. Except that it wasn't actually heroin, and I didn't exactly get busted."

"What happened?" Kiki asked, impressed that he was willing to admit to it outright.

"I did get arrested," Joshua explained, "but not because they thought I had drugs. I got arrested because I was driving home from a team party and I was pretty wasted. I pulled over to sleep it off. A cop knocked on my window about five in the morning. I had sobered up by then, but apparently you're not supposed to sleep in cars on the side of the road. I got a little angry, because I'd pulled over so I wouldn't endanger anyone, and here's a cop hassling me for it. We kind of got into it, so then they decided to search the car. They found a bag of creatine powder that I had because I was trying to bulk up, and assumed it was heroin. They eventually dropped all the charges, but that was about the worst hangover of my entire life." Josh laughed at the memory.

"So you didn't get sentenced to community service?"

"Of course not. Is that what you thought? That I had to do volunteer work?"

"Well, yeah, I wondered."

"I won't say that I'm only doing it out of the goodness of my heart. I've got some selfish reasons for doing it too. It will look great on my college applications. But no one makes me do it."

Kiki smiled. "Good to know."

Kiki's phone beeped, indicating an incoming text message.

"Oh my God! I forgot to tell Mark and Franklin that I'm not coming."

"So you guys are really close, huh?" he asked while she typed.

"Sometimes. It's like being a family. We fight a lot, but we're stuck together, so we have to work things out sooner or later."

"Like being on a team," he grinned.

"Exactly. Well, not exactly," she added. "If Franklin got wasted we would never let him drive anywhere."

Josh laughed, although Kiki wasn't kidding. "You don't understand," he explained. "I was probably the least toasted of the entire party. We were all really, really drunk."

"I figured." Kiki shared a few of her own Bad Things That Happen When You Drink stories, most of which involved her and Mark trying to save Franklin from fistfights with bouncers and angry boyfriends. They laughed all the way to Kiki's house.

Her mother had finished trimming the shrubs in front of the house, which meant she was tending to her precious rose garden in the backyard, getting the rose bushes ready for the winter. She always left the back door open when she gardened, just in case the house line rang, so Kiki elbowed Josh in the ribs when he practically screamed, "Where's the liquor cabinet?" as soon as they walked in.

"Shh," she hissed, jerking a thumb towards the kitchen. "My mom's around here somewhere."

"Where's the liquor cabinet?" he stage-whispered, wandering around the crowded living room curiously.

"My parents just drink wine."

"Wine rack?"

"In the kitchen, but they know how many bottles they have."

"I'm going on a beer run, then. What kind do you like?"

She shook her head in amazement. "Josh, it's one o'clock on a Sunday afternoon. Why are you in such a rush to start drinking?"

He looked equally confused. "It's Sunday afternoon—why wouldn't I be drinking?"

Kiki sank onto the couch. She couldn't believe she was having this discussion. She had just told him that her mother was there, and he wanted to go buy a six-pack? "If you go out that door to buy beer, don't bother coming back."

"What is your issue? The drink in your hand didn't bother you last night."

"There's a difference between drinking and being a drunk! I'd never drink so much that I would force a friend who didn't know anyone else at a party to find a ride home in the middle of the night. And I don't drive drunk either—even Franklin has never been that stupid. There is such a thing as drinking responsibly!"

"Fine," he said, heading for the door. "If you've got to judge everybody from your high-and-mighty point of view, be my guest! You're such a snob, Kiki. See you later."

Kiki was tempted to chase him out the door and explain exactly what it meant to be a snob, but it didn't seem worth it.

"So who's your friend?" her mother asked, popping her head into the living room.

"He's not my friend," Kiki said, closing her eyes wearily. "How much of that did you hear?"

"Everything from 'Wine rack?' on, I think." Kiki felt her mother settling onto the couch next to her.

"Am I grounded?"

"For drinking last night? You probably should be. You know how your father and I feel about that."

"Yeah, 'cause you guys never drank at all before you were legal."

Kiki's mother raised one carefully plucked eyebrow.

"Aunt Josephine told me about the night you two got trashed at Aunt Meredith's cotillion," Kiki said.

"*All* about that night?"

"Everything. Including the part where you disappear with Aunt Meredith's escort after drinking an entire bottle of champagne by yourself."

"That was your father," her mother said, blushing.

"Nope. You met Dad at Aunt Josephine's cotillion."

"You know that drinking is against the law, and that it would be very embarrassing for me if you were caught drinking. Not to mention bad for you," her mother said sternly. "On the other hand, I'm proud of you."

"Really?" Kiki examined her mother's face carefully to make sure she wasn't kidding. She had an odd sense of humor. But the smile on her face seemed to be all about love. "Why?"

"Because you didn't take a ride with someone who had been drinking. Because you called your friend out on what certainly sounds like some very problematic drinking habits. Because you actually know what it means to drink responsibly."

"So I'm not grounded?"

"No, you're not grounded." She slung an arm around Kiki's shoulders for a little half hug. "But if I hear you've been drinking again, I'll tell your father. And he doesn't need to hear about Aunt Meredith's cotillion, either."

Dumping Josh was definitely the right decision, even if Kiki doubted her choice. Turn to page 181 to find out what would have happened if Kiki had decided to stick with Josh, or to page 57 to choose another boy.

* Chapter 4 *

Michael

"Online dating just isn't for me," Kiki announced, leaning past Sasha to turn off the screen. "It's not like I really have time to date anyway."

"What do you mean?" Jasmine shrilled. "What are you so busy with now?"

"Physics," Kiki said, plopping back down on her bed. "And I have rehearsal at Franklin's in half an hour."

"Kind of late, isn't it?" Sasha asked, turning the screen back on to check the clock.

"Franklin had a doctor's appointment right after school."

"Checking on his venereal diseases?" Jasmine leered.

"You want to know the truth?" Kiki asked, putting her homework away.

"Well, duh!" Jasmine exclaimed.

"Franklin's at the dermatologist's."

The girls all gasped.

"But I've never even seen him with a pimple!" Sasha said.

"Not anymore. But apparently when he was in the eighth grade at Kenwood, they called him 'Spongeface.'"

"Well, what do you know?" Camille said, with a strangely thoughtful expression. Kiki had a bad feeling that Camille might actually give Franklin a chance.

"Don't start feeling sorry for him," Kiki warned her. "He's still a man-slut."

"But if he's only like that because kids used to make fun of him . . ."

"Don't be a doofus, Cam. Franklin isn't some tortured soul walking around in the body of a rock star. He's about as deep and complex as a sock puppet," Kiki pointed out. "But he is a nice guy." It was odd but true. Franklin had put his dweeby past behind him in a way that Mark never had, and probably never would. "And he's usually a lot of fun."

"Like Michael?" Sasha asked, raising one eyebrow.

"Yes, like Michael. But I never said I wanted to date Franklin either."

"Of course, Michael isn't riddled with disease," Sasha said. "Hopefully."

"Not that I'm ever going to find out. Seriously, guys, I can't go out with someone who—" Kiki was interrupted by her cell phone. "That'll be Mark. Time to roll."

"Can't," Sasha said, typing fast. "I'm working on an e-mail."

"You can e-mail Thomas from your house. I've got to run. Jasmine, what are you looking for in there?"

By the time Kiki had pried Sasha from the computer and Jasmine from her closet, Mark was waiting downstairs.

"Hello, Mark," Jasmine said, smirking. Kiki was beginning

to wonder if telling Jasmine that Mark was going to ask her out had been a good idea.

"Uh, hi, ladies," he said, turning a strange shade of red. "Kiki, you ready?"

"Sure. Everyone's leaving. Goodbye."

Kiki almost shoved the Pussycats out the door, not wanting to meet Camille and Sasha's curious stares—they were also trying to decide if Mark was actually interested in Jasmine.

The ride to Franklin's house wasn't comfortable. Mark was fidgeting with the steering wheel again, but he was talking, at least—this time, about their next album. They were going to spend Christmas break in the studio, two weeks of eighteen-hour days. They had to make every second count, since their next chance to do a major recording would be spring break, and the album was supposed to hit shelves in early May. They had done most of the writing over the summer, and they were already putting together scratch recordings for the label, but every song had to be session-ready by December 20. That was why Franklin had flipped out when Kiki skipped practice earlier that week, and why this was the worst possible time for the band to have relationship issues.

"Mark, try to chill," Kiki said when they arrived at Franklin's house. "Rock isn't supposed to sound uptight."

"It isn't supposed to sound bad either, which it will if we don't get in some practice time."

Franklin was noodling on his guitar when they walked into the music room, working on "Foxfire," which they also called "the song that never ends." They had been playing with it for more than six months. Everyone—the bandmates, A&R, even their managers—agreed that there was something there. Franklin's melody line was haunting, and the time signature—9/8, compound triple time—was more than weird enough to keep Kiki interested. But they had never come up with an arrangement everyone liked.

Halfway into this practice, Franklin started playing around with the lyrics to "Foxfire"—lyrics Mark had written—just to try something new. They played through to the end of the song, and instead of taking it again from the top, Mark stalked over to Franklin's music stand and ripped the battered notebook from it.

"Problem, Mark?" Franklin asked warily.

"I'm trying to see where that line about pale green eyes came from. I don't remember writing that line."

Kiki tucked her drumsticks into her waistband and sat back on her stool; she could tell this was going to take a minute.

"I just made it up, dude. The break is too boring without any vocal."

"You may think that your voice is necessary for every single measure, but some things sound better when you just shut up."

Franklin rolled his eyes in Kiki's direction, but she kept her mouth clamped shut. She had no desire to get involved.

"Dude, the break is boring. Either it needs some vocal, or something real interesting needs to happen in the melody line, or we should just cut it. But it's still not working the way it's written."

"Kiki, what do you think?" Mark asked in the false, sugary voice he sometimes used when he was trying not to scream.

"I think that I'm having some issues with the rhythm section. I don't like how the lead in—"

"I asked you about the break." He was squeezing his lyrics notebook so tightly his knuckles had turned white.

"And I am not going to fight with you two about it, unless you decide to make it a drum solo." Kiki shrugged and slumped farther back on her drum stool.

"Thanks for being so helpful. Do you realize we're supposed to be in the studio—"

"Yes, Mark, I do. But refusing to consider the possibility that Franklin might be right and you might be wrong, won't get us into the studio any faster."

"You would take his side," Mark growled.

"I'm not taking a side—I really don't know what to do to this song. I'm just suggesting that you listen to Franklin for once."

"If Franklin had one shred of musical theory to back up—" Mark paused when he noticed that Kiki was not only ignoring him but had actually gotten up to walk away.

"Where are you going?" he asked.

"I'm going upstairs to check my e-mail," she said, carefully clambering around her drum kit. The music room wasn't small, but the drums were crammed into a corner, and Kiki never got around to moving them. "Come and get me when you're ready to play."

"Kiki, this is no time to throw a temper tantrum."

"I'm not the one who's having a tantrum, Mark. I'm being serious. I don't know what to do about the song's structure, and I don't really care, beyond working out better beats. When you two have an arrangement you like, give me a call, then we can work on the percussion. But I am not going to be a part of another stupid argument."

Mark continued to whine, even as Kiki shut the door behind her very carefully, so that Mark couldn't accuse her of slamming it. After breathing deeply for thirty seconds and shaking the tension out of her shoulders, she wandered through arctic-white hallways and staircases to Franklin's filthy bedroom. Ignoring piles of clothes large enough to make her look like an infrequent shopper, she picked her way across the chaos to Franklin's desk. It was actually pretty clean, because Franklin rarely sat there longer than it took to check his friend requests on MySpace.

Kiki logged into her e-mail, and was surprised to see a message from someone called *mvideostar@telalink.net*. She assumed it had something to do with the video they did for "Friday Night Special"; otherwise she wouldn't have opened it.

"Hey," it began.

Thanks for e-mailing me. I know my profile says that I'm looking for more party buds, not a girlfriend, but when a rock star like you says hello, a guy reconsiders. If you need some good times, I'm your man. Are you busy tomorrow night?

—Michael

Kiki had speed-dialed Sasha before she finished reading the second sentence.

"I know what you're going to say," Sasha said, instead of hello.

"Actually, I'm pretty sure you don't know half of what I'm going to say, since I've learned more bad words from roadies than you picked up visiting churches with your grandma, but I think you're going to get my point," Kiki said through clenched teeth.

"Please don't be mad, Kiki. You know I don't like to meddle—"

"Then why did you?" Kiki screeched.

"Because sometimes the last thing you think you'd ever want is exactly what you need."

"So you think Michael and I are going to ride off into the sunset? Do you see marriage in our future?"

"No, but I think you'll have a good time with him. Don't you ever get tired of being serious all the time?"

"I'm a drummer, Sasha, not an executioner." She paused, then added, "I'm not Mark."

"Not yet. And don't tell me that you don't get tired of his all-work-no-play thing. I know you do. In fact, since you're reading e-mail in the middle of practice, my guess is that they're already driving you crazy. Let me guess: Mark thinks Franklin's being stupid, and Franklin thinks some rodent crawled up Mark's ass and died?"

Kiki let out a shaky laugh. "For someone who has never seen us practice, you know us pretty well."

"I know *you* well, Kiki. So why don't you trust me and give this thing with Michael a try? I'm not saying it's going to be everlasting love, but one date isn't going to kill you."

"If it does, I'll haunt you forever, Sasha Silverman."

She laughed. "Jews don't believe in ghosts, Kiki. At least I don't think we do."

"Well, I'm not Jewish, so I don't think it matters," Kiki said.

"So you aren't going to kill me for using your e-mail address?"

"Not until I actually go out with this Michael guy. If he sucks, then I'll kill you."

"All right. I'll be keeping my fingers crossed."

"Good. That way you can't type any more e-mail from my address."

After Kiki told Sasha goodbye, she e-mailed Michael, then rejoined her bandmates downstairs. They were completely silent when she let herself back into the room.

"Are you two finished fighting?" she asked, working her way back toward the drum stool.

"We're canceling the recording session Saturday night. And I think we're cutting the break," Mark said tightly.

"Fine. Then let's get back to work."

The next day's practice went much more smoothly, possibly because Kiki was working extra-hard to keep everyone on task. They were finished promptly at 7:30.

"Want to pick up some dinner on the way home?" Mark asked, loosening the strings on his Stratocaster.

"Nah. I've got a ride."

"Hot date?" he asked sarcastically. There was nothing unusual about Mark being snarky when he didn't really mean it, and Kiki had been called the Queen of Snark herself. Still, Kiki thought she heard the faintest undertone of anger in Mark's voice.

"Actually, yes, Mark. But I don't see why that's a problem. It's not like we've ever gone out. And anyway, I thought you were going out with Jasmine."

Franklin almost tripped over his own guitar stand.

"You're going out with the Bloom of Doom?" he gasped.

"I was going to ask her to Trip-Hop Triple Threat this Friday, unless someone's got a problem with that."

Franklin held up both hands and said, "I'm just warning you, man. I talked to Jerry Ryan, who went out with her most of last year. That's one girl who'll hand you your balls if you piss her off."

"Jazz isn't that bad," Kiki insisted. "You just have to keep her entertained. And you can't take her too seriously."

"That's it—you're doomed. Don't talk to her, man."

"You can't tell me what to do, Franklin."

Kiki walked out, knowing that the fight would go on and on, and it would be pointless. Mark would win, arguing Franklin into the ground, but there was no way he would ask Jasmine out now: Mark could probably deal with Jasmine, but having to listen to Franklin's mockery would drive him crazy. But the truth was, Franklin was right: Jasmine and Mark were not meant to be. Opposites might attract, if you were talking about magnets, but not usually with people. That kind of thing worked better in the movies than it did in real life, which was why Kiki was more than a little worried when a battered Thunderbird, held together with duct tape, rolled into Franklin's pristine white driveway.

The car's top was down, and since Franklin's house was surrounded by security lights, Kiki got a good look at Michael. And one look was enough to ensure that she would definitely be getting into his car. Catnip for girls, Sasha had called him—and she was right. But it was more than just the eyes, green as playing fields, and the curly, soft hair. More than the broad shoulders under his jean jacket, which looked butter-soft from washing and perfectly worn in. More than the face that might have belonged to a very tolerant angel. Michael had a smile that made all the clenched muscles in Kiki's shoulders and back instantly relax. It was better than a massage.

"Hey!" he said, waving, but not getting out of the car. "Nice place!"

"This isn't my house. I just practice here. Didn't I say that in my e-mail?"

"Oh yeah. You did." He slapped himself on the forehead. "I've killed a lot of brain cells recently."

Kiki opened the passenger-side door cautiously. She had thought that Mark's car was in bad shape, but it was just old. His parents had babied it for the last thirty years. This car looked like someone had attacked it with a baseball bat. And, as it turned out, someone had.

"Sorry about the car. I was driving home from a friend's cabin one weekend, out near Lieper's Fork, when we noticed that this pickup truck was following us. No big deal, we thought—he was probably just headed back to Nashville. But when we turned off on Old Hickory, to get to my friend's house, he was still behind us. Then we turn onto Steeplechase, and there he was. It was weird. So I pulled over, and he pulled over, and I went over to his car and asked if there was a problem. He said, 'You skipped me at a four-way stop.' And I was like, 'Dude, no I didn't. And so what if I did?' And that's when the bat came out."

"Oh my God!" Kiki said, though the hand over her mouth muffled her exclamation. "What did you do?"

"Well, there wasn't a whole lot I could do. I mean, he had a bat! Leslie and I just stood there and watched for a minute, then we started cheering. Really whooping it up—'Go, dude! You're the man! Show that car who's boss!' She was doing high kicks and everything. It kind of freaked him out, I think. He took off pretty soon after that."

"You didn't call the police?"

"Well, that was a few months before I got my license."

"Are you kidding?"

"'Fraid not. But it was all right in the end. My friend Marco lifted the dude's license plate while Leslie and I were acting a fool—bet he didn't get back to Lieper's Fork without a ticket."

Kiki's laughter was half-horrified, half-amazed. That kind of thing never happened to anyone she knew.

"And that's not even the craziest thing that's happened to me in this car."

By the time they pulled onto the interstate, Kiki could barely breathe, she was laughing so hard. Michael's life was an endless stream of crazy parties, attempts to evade angry parents and dumb cops, and surprising adventures in the woods, occasionally interrupted by school. It couldn't be more different from her life, but it did sound like fun.

"So where are we going? To a party?" she shouted over the wind.

His answer was muffled, but she thought she caught the word "arcade."

"The Arcade? Downtown? I've been to some of the art galleries there with my mom." She had even run into one of her managers there, at an opening at Twist. It was the only time she had ever seen Frederick in jeans.

Kiki could hear Michael's laugh, despite the rushing air. "Not The Arcade. An arcade. You know: video games, bad pizza?"

"I'm familiar with the concept," she yelled. "But I haven't been to one in years."

"Really?" He seemed genuinely shocked. "That's terrible!" He gunned the engine, as if they had no time to waste.

The arcade was half empty when they arrived. The cheesiest pop music ever recorded blared through speakers, competing with the theme music from driving games, shooting games, and every other kind of video game. Popcorn was ground into the hideous turquoise carpet, and the whole place reeked of burned pizza. But, icky as it was, it wasn't half as nasty as some of the clubs where Kiki had played.

"Come on," Michael said, taking Kiki by the hand. "I'm going to teach you how to drive."

So you do remember something about the e-mail I sent, Kiki thought. *You've got to have a brain cell or two in there somewhere.*

He also had really, really good reflexes. Kiki totaled her virtual Lamborghini halfway into her her first trip through the winding roads of *Ultimate Drag Racing—Level One: California, Route 1,* while Michael easily conquered the first level.

"Aren't you going to keep going?" Kiki asked when he clambered out of his seat.

"No, you slide over. Hurry, or I'll have to put in another quarter."

She did, and destroyed his Ferrari in about three minutes.

"Maybe it's a good thing you don't have a license," he said with a wink and that bone-melting smile of his.

"If you drove like that in the real world, you wouldn't have a license either, for long."

"Who says I do?"

Kiki's eyes widened in shock.

"I'm kidding, Kiki," Michael said, laughing. "Kidding! Stop looking at me like that!"

She poked him in the side. "Let's play something where I can't get killed."

"How about 'Deer Hunter'? It's pretty straightforward."

"I'm a vegetarian. I can't shoot deer, even virtual ones."

He patted the side of her face. "Honey, I'm pretty sure you aren't going to kill any deer."

It took $2.75 and lots and lots of coaching, but Kiki did eventually shoot a deer.

"Good for you! High five!"

She slapped his hand, but she couldn't match his excitement.

"But that was a doe. Instant 'game over.'"

"Well, yeah, but still—you hit it! You rock!"

"You're crazy," she said, shaking her head.

"Crazy in love." He swooped down and kissed her before she could call him a liar. It was just a peck on the lips, but it left her wanting more.

"Hey, everybody!" he shouted to handful of thirteen-year-olds and the bored arcade attendants. "I'm on a date with a rock star! Isn't she amazing!"

He clapped and whooped until everyone in the room joined in, cheering, even though they probably had no idea who she was. Michael's cheer was infectious, almost impossible to resist. Kiki could feel her cheeks burning, but what could she do? Besides, she was having huge fun.

"Ah. Um. Thanks, everybody." She took a quick bow, then dashed over to the Ball Crawl to hide from the now curious video game junkies.

Michael followed her, and plunged into the pool of smooth plastic balls like a kid belly-flopping into a lake.

"Good call," he said, wading over to Kiki. "Private, comfortable, a bit old-fashioned, but still entertaining."

"You really are insane, aren't you?" she asked, grinning. She stood in the middle with her arms folded across her chest. "The walls are made of nets. You can see right through them."

"Yeah. So lie down. Come on. It's fun! The six-year-olds do it all the time!"

He demonstrated, half-burying himself. She went ahead and joined him when she felt his fingers winding around her ankle. Better to just lie down than be yanked down. Faster than Kiki could crash a racecar, Michael had crawled close enough for a kiss. This was the real thing, tongues slipping playfully past lips and teeth. Kiki didn't know how long it would take for things to progress a little further—not long, she was sure—but one of the arcade attendants without much to do kept clearing his throat just outside the Ball Crawl. Michael seemed all set to ignore him, and Kiki was enjoying the whole go-with-the-flow thing herself, until the attendant finally said, "Excuse me, but there's no making out in the Ball Crawl."

He sounded so completely uncomfortable, Kiki couldn't help laughing.

"Actually, there is," Michael pointed out without moving an inch away from Kiki. "So if you could go find something else to do—"

"It's in the rules, sir."

"Oh really?" Michael finally sat up, while Kiki rolled around, giggling madly. "Where does it say no making out? I've seen the rules—they're posted right outside the door. And it definitely doesn't say 'No making out.'"

"It says 'No inappropriate behavior.'"

"And if your date looked like her, what do you think would be appropriate?"

"Okay, Michael, stop baiting him," Kiki said, getting shakily to her knees. She was still breathless from laughter. "Let's go somewhere more appropriate."

"As you wish." He attempted to bow and managed to keel over, back into the balls.

"Come on, you," she said, hauling him to his feet. As soon as it was clear that they really weren't going to have sex in the arcade, the attendant went back to his station at the game counter. On the way out the door, Kiki noticed that he was blushing from the neck up.

"Time to hit a few parties anyway, I guess," Michael said as they got to his car. "I know about three big ones and a couple of intimate gatherings. Unimpressive, I know, but it's Wednesday. Not a great night for parties."

"You know I have to be home at ten-thirty right?" Kiki said, checking the clock on her cell phone. It was already 9:25.

"That wasn't a joke?"

"I wish. My parents don't mess around, either. One second late and I'm grounded."

"Wow." He made a face. "Well, we've got time for one, at least."

They belted themselves in, and after a few tries the engine turned over. They were flying north on the interstate a few minutes later, in the opposite direction from Kiki's house.

"I really do need to get home by ten-thirty!" she shouted.

"Don't worry about it! I just need to drop by and say hello to a couple of people!"

Kiki didn't answer—she was already tired of yelling. She was worried, and she worried more with every mile-marker they passed. There were a lot of them. They didn't get off the interstate until they were well past the city, getting close to Percy Priest Lake.

"That's where we're going," Michael responded to her nervous question. "One of my friends has a houseboat."

"Why would someone who lived out here go to your high school?" she asked. She didn't know much about public schools, but she knew there had to be several between Percy Priest Lake and Hillsboro High School, where Michael went.

"Oh, he's not in high school. He's got to be twenty-something."

"What does he do?" Kiki asked. When she was sixteen, the only twenty-somethings she knew were in the music industry.

"You know," he said slowly, "I have no idea. Remind me to ask when we get there."

But when they arrived at the party, Kiki didn't have a chance to remind Michael of anything. A bouncy blond person threw herself into his arms, spilling half her beer on one of Kiki's shoes.

"Michael! I haven't seen you in ages! Where have you been?"

"Here and there, Kara. Here and there. Hey, I want you to meet—"

"I haven't seen you since Leslie's birthday party. She's going to kill you for disappearing like that." She pulled out of his hug just far enough to punch him in the shoulder. "Leslie! Hey, Leslie! Look who's here!"

"MICHAEL!" Another blonde launched herself at Michael. Somehow Kiki found herself standing on a deck, completely surrounded by drunken strangers, at 9:52 PM. Lots of drunken strangers. There had to be at least fifty people packed onto the deck of a boat meant to hold twenty on a good day.

"Hey there, cutie. Want a beer?" asked a guy who looked about her age, though she wasn't sure. The only light came from the full moon in the clear night sky. It was a typical October night—not cold, exactly, but not warm either. She was wearing a sweater, and she was beginning to wish for a real jacket.

"No thanks. I'm going to have a hard enough time explaining to my father why my left foot smells like beer. Did you see where Michael went?"

"He went with the ladies," the stranger said, wandering off.

Kiki sighed, pushed her hair behind her ears, then started shoving her way through the crowd. He couldn't have gone that far; after all, they were on a boat. When the rumble of talk and laughter on the other side of the boat rose to a new level,

Kiki sensed something bad was about to happen. Then she heard splashes, and the sound of people cheering.

"Yeah," she muttered to herself. "That was it."

By the time she made it to where the crowd was thickest, she could see what was happening: several guys had stripped down to their boxers for a quick swim to the other side of the lake. She didn't need to track the swimmers with a flashlight, like some of the girls were doing, to know that Michael was out there somewhere.

"What happened to their clothes?" Kiki asked a pretty redhead who had just finished throwing up over the side of the boat.

"They put them over there, so they wouldn't get stepped on." The girl pointed a shaky finger at a pile of coiled rope. Sure enough, tucked inside, Kiki found several pairs of jeans, T-shirts, and sneakers. She found Michael's without too much trouble, tucked them under her arm, and headed back toward the dock.

"Where are you going?" asked the same guy who had spoken to her earlier.

"Tell Michael I'm going home." She stomped across the wooden gangplank to Michael's car, and very nearly got into the driver's seat. She knew, though, that however angry her parents would be if she missed curfew, it would be gumdrops and candy canes compared to how they would react to a phone call from the cops informing them that their unlicensed daughter, reeking of beer, had been pulled over in a car registered to someone else. "Bad scene" didn't begin to cover it. So she pulled up the ragtop, got in, locked the doors, and waited.

Fortunately, just a few minutes later Michael came jogging over to the car, trailed by the sound of laughter from the boat.

"Where are my clothes? Hey, why is the door locked?" he asked, hopping from foot to foot.

"You drive me home right now, and maybe I'll tell you where I put your clothes!"

"Fine, whatever. Just let me in. I'm freezing!"

"Promise me you'll drive straight home!" Kiki shouted. She hated to waste even a second, but she couldn't afford for him to decide to stop by another party to say hello.

"I promise!" he shrieked, jumping up and down. "I swear!"

"I bet." Kiki reached across the car to open his door. He hopped in, slammed the door, and gave Kiki another quick kiss. It was so fast she didn't have time to resist.

"There. I'm feeling nice and toasty. Now, let's get you home in a hurry."

Kiki had to fight a smile. His good-natured energy was infectious. And he really was ready to drive clear across town in a drafty convertible, wearing only soaking-wet boxers. Kiki now had a very clear idea of what she was missing by demanding a ride home. If she had any doubts about Michael's popularity with girls, she had lost them with one look at his nearly naked form. She couldn't even imagine what Jasmine would say if she were here.

On the ride home, Michael kept the radio tuned to what she and Mark called the "soccer mom station," all cheesy pop, all the time. Still, Kiki was too worried to complain. She thought that she would either get home after 10:30 or, because of Micael's speed, wind up wrapped around a tree, completely unrecognizable. She was terrified all the way around.

They screeched into her driveway at 10:29:42, and Kiki was pelting for the door before the car had completely stopped.

"I'll call you tomorrow!" Michael shouted after her.

"Fine!" She was concentrating on getting her key into the lock, but wasn't surprised when the doorknob turned before she could get it in. Both of her parents were frowning, looking entirely serious despite her father's ridiculously ratty robe and her mother's curlers.

"Hey, Kiki!" Michael called from the street. "Where did you put my clothes?!"

Kiki cringed and watched her parents exchange a look. It was not a good look, either.

Without turning around, she shouted back, "They're under your seat, Michael. Goodnight."

"Cool! See ya!"

"Kiki, did some naked man just drive you home late?" her father asked, sounding amazed.

"Not exactly," she mumbled. "I still had eight seconds."

"And why was he naked?" her mother asked.

"Because he was swimming in Percy Priest."

"Kiki, of course you're in trouble for being late, but you know not to lie," her mother said irritably.

"Oddly enough, I'm not lying. He really was swimming in Percy Priest. And I'm really not late." She showed them her cell phone, which showed a time of 10:30:07.

"But it's freezing! And heaven knows what's in that water."

"Yeah, he's insane. Could you let me in? It is kind of cold out here."

After a brief argument about the exact time of her return, which Kiki actually won, she typed up a quick description of her date and e-mailed it to Sasha, Camille, and Jasmine. She had answers from all three of them within half an hour. *Silver-*

Michael

Sasha@nashville.goth.net said, "What a moron! He just left you standing there? I'm sorry I e-mailed him in the first place. You can chop off my big toe as punishment." *Bloomofdoom@-belloftn.com* said, "Don't forget how much fun you had before the party. That was still the best date you've had in the last year, I bet. (And if you dump him before you've seen him completely nude, you're an idiot.) *Camstersrgoodpets@sffgst.net* said, "I don't know what to think about this guy. What do you think?"

"Good question," Kiki muttered aloud. "What do I think about Michael?"

"He's a loser!" a voice called from the hallway. "Never go out with him again."

"Thanks, Mom. But I wasn't asking you."

SHOULD KIKI TRY HIM ON?
Turn to page 219 to see if Michael's her perfect fit.

❤

SHOULD KIKI PUT HIM BACK ON THE RACK?
Turn to page 229 to see what happens if she tells him goodbye.

✳ Chapter 5 ✳

The Zombies

"**S**ure I'd like to go out again," Kiki said, after switching her cell phone from one ear to the other. Before Michael got around to asking her out, he had babbled on and on about how much fun she had missed the night before. She'd already missed half her lunch break and was afraid that she was going to spend all of it on the phone in the second floor girls' bathroom. "But I'd rather do something a little more structured next time, you know?"

"What do you mean?" Michael seemed genuinely confused by the word "structured." Kiki wasn't surprised.

"I mean, dinner and a movie. Dinner and dancing. You know. A real date." A couple of freshman girls walked in, giggling about something. Kiki raised an eyebrow in their general direction, pointed at her cell phone, and they headed back out again.

"No problem. My buddy was telling me about this B-movie marathon out at the drive-in, in Watertown. *Creature from the*

Black Lagoon, Plan 9 from Outer Space, that kind of thing. They're hilarious, even if you aren't stoned."

"That sounds . . . interesting," she said. She had never actually seen a B-movie, but she had heard about them, and had seen references to them in other movies. She would much rather see a good live band than *Attack of the 50 Foot Woman*, but all relationships involve a little compromise. "I guess I'm game. How far away is Watertown?" Going to the Watertown drive-in was one of those things that people always talked about doing, but no one ever did. At least, no one Kiki knew had been there. It was a nice idea, though—cuddling in Michael's Thunderbird, which looked like it might have been around since before there *were* drive-ins, watching silly black-and-white movies about monsters. It would be more interesting than going to Laura Keller's party, which is what Kiki would be doing otherwise.

"Oh, like forty minutes, or something," Michael said. "It starts at sundown and goes on all night, but if we get bored, we can always hit some parties."

"Okay. Sounds good. Do you want to do dinner before, or pick up something to eat at the drive-in?"

"I don't know. What do you think?"

"We should probably bring something. It gets dark right at five, which is a little early for dinner."

"Okay. Want me to pick you up at seven?"

Kiki sighed inwardly. "Well, sundown is at five. If you want to see the first movie, we should leave around four. But if you don't care which movies we see, seven should be fine."

"Great! See you at seven!"

After they said goodbye, Kiki dashed downstairs and outside to the football field. The Pussycats were sitting at the top of the stands, as far from the school building as they possibly could. Kiki managed to shove half a slice of cold pizza in her mouth before anyone could ask where she had been.

"Starving," she mumbled. "Talk later."

"Come on, dude. You're not getting off that easily," Jasmine smirked. "Were you in a broom closet with Mark?"

"Nah. Still over him." Strangely enough, it was almost true this time. It still hurt a little to think that he just wasn't interested, despite everything they shared, but maybe a relationship with him really wouldn't have worked out in the end. Dating really was supposed to be fun. Dating Mark might be intense and interesting and, well, hot, but it wouldn't be a lot of fun. She should have realized this a long time ago. Just because someone is a good friend doesn't mean they would be a good boyfriend; denim is great for jeans and jackets, comfy things you wear every day, but you wouldn't use it for a formal gown, or socks, and definitely not for your underwear.

"She was in the second floor bathroom, on the phone," Camille said without looking up from the remains of her spinach salad. Kiki gave her a piercing glare over her pizza, but Camille just shrugged. "Abby saw you. She wanted to know what was up."

Kiki slapped her forehead, thinking, that's what you get for thinking of freshmen as little people who just get in the way, without names and brains of their own. Abby was Camille's little sister, but her mouth wasn't any smaller than Cam's.

Sasha and Jasmine both narrowed their eyes, looking at Kiki with consideration. They looked at each other, then said, "Michael," at the same time, like twins. But they said it in very different tones of voice. Sasha sounded horrified; Jasmine sounded amused.

"No comment," Kiki said, taking a bite out of her daily Granny Smith.

"Oh, come on," Jasmine said. "Tell us what's up. Are you bringing him to Laura Keller's party?"

"That'll be a no."

"You're not going to tell us?" Sasha asked.

"Nope."

"Meanie!" Jasmine said, shaking a finger at her.

"Get over yourself, Jazz. If you wanted him so badly, you could have gotten into this boy-shopping thing yourself."

Jasmine stuck out her lower lip in a textbook pout. It looked like something she'd practiced in the mirror, and, knowing Jasmine, she probably had.

"Don't worry, Jasmine," Sasha said, sounding rather worried herself. "I bet Michael will be back on the market sooner or later. Probably sooner."

Oddly, that made Kiki even more determined to make it work. So when Michael was fifteen minutes late picking her up, she didn't give him the lecture that was boiling away inside her. Instead she kissed him lightly, lingering just a bit on his sensuous lower lip and said, "I packed us sandwiches and drinks, so we don't need to stop anywhere."

"Hey, cool! You're so good at this planning-ahead thing." Michael backed out of Kiki's driveway so fast he nearly hit their neighbor's mailbox, causing Kiki to claw four new quarter-moon-shaped holes in the armrest, joining an untold number of cigarette burns and holes of more mysterious origins.

"Um, yes, I am. But it's not like I have a lot of choice about that," she pointed out, gently prying her fingernails out of the armrest.

"Wow! Your parents really get on your case, huh?"

"Not so much them as my managers. It drives them crazy that we're at school forty hours a week. They've been begging me and Mark's parents to let us go to online high school for years."

Michael looked at her so long she was afraid he was going to hit something. "There's high school on the *Internet*? You can do that?"

Kiki sighed and steered the conversation toward his adventures in public school. It had always seemed exciting in comparison to Wentworth, where there weren't a lot of rules, since no one ever did anything especially rebellious. Michael's high school sounded insane: people set things on fire, had ultimate Frisbee games on the roof during assemblies, and gambled fifty- and hundred-dollar bills on girl fights in the cafeteria.

"And you would rather go to school at home?" Kiki asked, completely baffled.

They compared schools all the way to Watertown, which was a lot farther than forty minutes away. Kiki was worried that they would have to park so far from the screen that they wouldn't be able to tell the Martians from the zombies. Instead, Michael was able to pull up right in front of the screen, because there was nothing showing there at all.

"That's weird," Michael said, peering around at the eerily empty field. It was full dark, but the giant screen glowed palely in the moonlight. A faded sign taped to the box office, a tiny building next to the driveway, said,

END OF SUMMER FESTIVAL: B MOVIE MARATHON!
LABOR DAY WEEKEND, SEPTEMBER 4-6!
LAST CHANCE TO ENJOY THE DRIVE-IN THIS YEAR!

"Weird is one word for it," Kiki said, doing the breathing exercise one of her managers taught everyone on the Temporary Insanity tour bus. It was supposed to keep them from screaming at one another. This time, it worked.

Once Kiki was sure she was not going to raise her voice, she said, "You didn't check to see when the film festival was going on?"

"Neither did you," Michael pointed out. Kiki had to admit that this was true. If she was going to date Michael, it was clear that she was going to be the one who kept track of things. She should have realized it the day they met.

"Okay, good point. So, now what? I know about a party going on in Belle Meade."

He made a face. "Belle Meade? They've got police every-where."

"You weren't planning to do anything very illegal, were you?" Kiki asked. "I mean, you do sober up before you drive. Right?"

"Well, yeah. Of course I do. But Belle Meade cops don't need an excuse to pull you over. They just do it."

"But if you can pass the Breathalyzer, what difference does it make?"

He shifted uncomfortably in his seat. "I may have some un-paid tickets hanging around."

Alarm bells went off in the back of Kiki's mind. They

sounded a lot like her mother's keys jingling in the morning, except they rang out, *Unpaid tickets can mean a revoked license. Driving on a revoked license means a trip to jail!*

"Okay . . ." Kiki said slowly. "Laura Keller's might not be the best place for you to be. The Jennifers are playing at the End. They're pretty awesome. Want to check it out?"

"I don't really like live music," he said without looking up from his cell phone. He was tapping out a text message, which Kiki knew was some variation on, "Who's throwing a party tonight?"

"You don't like live music?" Kiki repeated, hoping she had misunderstood him somehow.

"Nah. You've got to sneak in, get the bartender to serve you, you can't really meet anybody because of all the noise."

"And by noise you mean music?" Kiki was having a hard time wrapping her brain around the not-liking-music concept. To her mind, it was like saying, "I don't like oxygen."

"Yeah, music. I mean, yeah, it's cool if you're dancing or something, but dance clubs have a cover, and the drinks are pricy. But basically the music is just background noise for the real stuff that's happening."

If Michael had started spouting religious philosophy, Kiki could not have been more shocked.

"Um, Michael, I think maybe you ought to take me home."

"Why? It's not even nine o'clock."

"I don't think we have anything in common."

He looked as shocked as Kiki had felt a moment before. "What do you mean? We've got lots of stuff in common!"

"Like what?"

225

"We both like to party, B-movies, video games—"

"Yep, time to go home."

"Is this about the music thing?"

Kiki shut her eyes and did a few more deep-breathing exercises. Michael really was a nice guy, and she didn't want to hurt his feelings. But he was like a zombie that had come back from the dead to party rather than eat brains. It wasn't hard to imagine him stumbling around, moaning, "Paaaaaarty! Paaaaaaaarty!" In fact, he was probably like that every morning around 3:00.

"Michael, I really think I need to be getting home. I have a lot of work to do."

"On a Saturday night?"

"I always have a lot of work to do."

"Wow. Bummer." Disappointed as he was, he started the car and pulled out of the deserted drive-in.

When they were near Kiki's house, Michael said, "So I guess we're going to just be friends, right?"

"Sure," Kiki agreed.

"Friends with benefits?"

She had to laugh. "Not a chance. But, hey, I'll call you sometime."

He pouted, reminding her of Jasmine, and Kiki laughed again.

"Goodbye," she said a few moments later, kissing him on the cheek. "Take it easy."

"I always take it easy." He grinned. "See you around." Once again, he backed perilously out of her driveway and drove off into the night.

The Zombies

Grinning to herself, Kiki pulled out her cell phone. "Hey, Jazz," she said. "Want to give me a ride to Laura's party?"

That didn't work out as well as Kiki might have hoped. To see what would have happened if Kiki had decided to dump Michael, turn to page 229. To try another boy, turn to page 57.

Think that Michael is more trouble than pr
Read on to find out what happens when
dump him!

* **Chapter 5** *

Why Can't We Be Friends?

"**F**riends with benefits?" Michael asked hopefully when Kiki told him she just wanted to be friends.

"No, no benefits. Just friends." A pair of giggling freshman girls wandered into the second floor girls' bathroom, where Kiki had gone to keep this conversation private. Kiki raised an eyebrow in their general direction, pointed at her cell phone, and they trooped back out.

"Oh. Well. Friends. That's cool. Want to come over tonight and play *Kill the Earthlings*?"

Kiki slapped her forehead in frustration. "I just said that I just want to be friends!"

"Exactly. Friends play video games together. That's how it works. You bring some friends. I bring some friends. Everyone becomes friends. It's called 'social networking.' It's cool. It's the reason I signed up for HelloHello."

Kiki was surprised that he was taking her at her word—most people seemed to think that "Let's be friends" meant "I never want to speak to you again." She was even more sur-

.ed that Michael knew what the phrase "social networking" .neant.

"Er, okay. I have band practice, but I guess I could come over later."

"Excellent! I'll e-mail you directions! See you later!"

Kiki wandered out to the football field in a daze. She found the Pussycat Posse sitting at the top of the bleachers, as far away from the school buildings as they could get without leaving campus.

"You know how you can try to dump somebody and it doesn't exactly work?" she asked, fishing her cold pizza out of a tin Pink Floyd lunchbox that was older than she was.

"You mean you just couldn't say it?" Camille asked sympathetically. She was always having to find nice ways to let boys down. It was more than just her girl-next-door blond beauty, which was less striking than the other, black-clad Pussycats. Camille was so nice that she hated to break up with guys, no matter how much she wanted to do it. That was one reason she was the most popular member of the Pussycat Posse, at least with guys.

"No . . . Not exactly. I mean, he knows we're not going out anymore, but now I have to go play video games at his house with his friends." She took a bite of pizza, looked thoughtful, then added, "You guys have to come too."

If Kiki had said, "You guys all have to shave your heads now," she could not have gotten a noisier response. But after all the shouting, Camille, Jasmine and Sasha had all agreed to go, as long as Sasha could bring Thomas.

* * *

Kiki had no idea what to expect when Jasmine pulled into Michael's driveway, which was connected to a perfectly normal ranch-style house in Brentwood, a suburb south of the city. Kiki had imagined that Michael's parents were spaced-out wrecks, or maybe didn't exist at all, but an ordinary brown-haired woman with her son's brilliant green eyes and laid-back smile let the girls in.

"Brownies are in the oven," she said with a twinkly, toothpaste-commercial smile. "Everyone else is downstairs in the rec room."

After thanking her, the Pussycats and Thomas ventured down the stairs, expecting hashish smoke, hard liquor, and mayhem. They did find mayhem, in the form of seven or eight teenagers, yelling and laughing, playing a video game based on B-movies from the 1950s. A virtual Michael, who looked like a small green alien, was chasing goats around a field with a ray gun until an angry farmer shot him.

"Oh well," he shrugged, handing his controller to the pretty brunette sitting next to him.

"Hi, Michael," Kiki said from the staircase.

"Oh, hey! Kiki! I'm glad you made it! And you brought friends!" He picked his way around sprawling bodies to give her a friendly hug. They introduced everyone around, and somehow the evening evolved into a boys-versus-girls video showdown. Jasmine managed to take down two capital cities, more than anyone else, winning the contest for the girls.

"So what's your pleasure?" Michael asked Jasmine, staring directly into her eyes. "If you want to make us your sex slaves for a day, that would be perfectly fine with me."

"You wish," said his brunette friend, whose name turned out to be Lisa, elbowing him in the ribs. She and Kiki had immediately bonded when Michael said something unbelievably stupid about live music, and they both had to hit him over the head with a throw pillow. One of his guy friends, George, stepped on his foot, earning him a grin from Kiki.

"I have a suggestion," said Molly, another one of Michael's female friends. "How about a night of no games? We could go dancing, or catch a show, or even go ice-skating or something. But no games and no parties!"

"But I hate live music," Michael whined, forcing Kiki to hit him again. "And you can't drink at the skating rink. It's all ages."

"I haven't been ice-skating in forever," Jasmine said. "Let's do it."

So the next night, the Pussycat Posse, Molly, and Lisa gathered at Kiki's house, then carpooled over to the Sportsplex, Nashville's only ice-skating rink. They expected the boys to stand them up, but the boys actually had arrived first, and let them cut in line.

"I can't believe you thought we wouldn't come," Michael said, clutching a part of his chest that he probably thought was close to his heart. "We take our games very seriously."

"I know," Molly said, punching him in the shoulder. "It's about the only thing you do take seriously."

Once they got on the ice, Kiki began to wonder if this was such a good idea after all. Her friends were the oldest people on the ice, and they fell more often than most of the kids. But before long everyone was having fun, singing along with the terrible pop music pumped over the radio, laughing at one another when they fell, which was rarer and rarer for everyone except Jasmine. Every time Michael came near her, she wiped out, and Michael had to tenderly help her up.

Kiki caught Lisa's eye and grinned. She nodded, and began to skate a little faster, executing little turns and quick stops just when Jasmine let go of the rail, startling her every time. Poor Jasmine! Michael helped her off the ice and bought her some hot chocolate. Soon the two of them were huddled over an ancient sit-down *Ms. Pac-Man* game, distracting one another.

Kiki had to laugh. Boy shopping was no different from clothes shopping: every strange-colored sweater, oddly cut pair of pants, and silly, bright pattern was perfect for somebody. Michael was definitely not right for Kiki, but he just might be Jasmine's perfect fit. If there was one thing Kiki knew about shopping, it was that you didn't settle for something that wasn't quite right. You just had to keep on looking until you found what was right for you.

"You going to stand there watching them all night?" George asked, skating up to Kiki.

"No way!" She held out her hand, and the two of them joined the whirling, giggling throng, skating to their own beat.

Michael might not have been right for Kiki, but someone else might be! Go back to page 57 and choose a new boy for our girl.